DRAGGED
FROM UNDER

THE GREAT WHITE SHARK

DRAGGED FROM UNDER

DRAGGED FROM UNDER

THE GREAT WHITE SHARK

Joseph Monninger

Scholastic Inc.

Text copyright © 2021 by Joseph Monninger
Photos © Shutterstock: cover font and throughout (zphoto), i-iii (solarseven), 43, 82, 126 (Sloth Astronaut).

While inspired by real events and historical characters, this is a work of fiction and does not claim to be historically accurate or portray factual events or relationships. Please keep in mind that references to actual persons, living or dead, business establishments, events, or locales may not be factually accurate, but rather fictionalized by the author.

ISBN 978-1-338-58771-5

10 9 8 7 6 5 4 3 2 1   21 22 23 24 25

Printed in the U.S.A.   40
First printing 2021

Book design by Stephanie Yang

For Heather

There were sharks before there were dinosaurs, and the reason there are still sharks in the ocean is that nothing is better at being a shark than a shark.

—Douglas Adams

Interesting fact: A shark will only attack you if you're wet.

—Anonymous

PROLOGUE

First Attack

Jimmy Xanthopoulous waded into the Atlantic slowly. He felt sleepy and hungry, and he didn't know what he was doing going surfing so early in the morning. His board—a Channel Islands Fred Rubble board, perfect for the waist-high waves of Cape Cod—felt heavy in his arms. He dropped the board softly on the wash of the last wave and felt the board immediately tug at the tether attached to his left ankle.

"Yo, yo, yo," he heard someone call.

It sounded like his brother, Dimitri, who was already in the water and already looking for his first set.

The sound of his brother's voice blended with the calls of gulls.

For a second wave, Jimmy did nothing but try to wake up. That wasn't easy. He had worked the dead man's shift at his father's pizza parlor the night before, and after cleanup and prep for the morning crew, he had not left the parlor until close to 2:00 a.m. Now it was 8:27, gray, quiet, soft. Cold for early June. He had slept fewer than five hours.

That wasn't enough.

That wasn't close to enough.

He bent down and splashed his face. The water pushed him awake a little more. The cold seeping into his wet suit made him shiver. He tasted salt on his lips.

Before he lunged forward to get paddling, he saw Dimitri rise up on a wave. That was a kind of magic. People could go from sitting on their boards to standing in an instant. He loved that about surfing. Dimitri was not very good—he was more enthusiastic than skilled—but he stood on a wave—a surfing god, he would say—and flicked the front of his board back and forth to keep his balance.

"You coming or not?" Dimitri yelled when he finally bailed on the ride.

He hadn't gotten far. Not a great ride. Dimitri never got a great ride, but that didn't kill his juice for it.

"It's cold, and I'm tired," Jimmy called back.

"Get into it. You'll be all right."

Dimitri began paddling back through the surf. Jimmy watched him. He loved his brother, admired him, emulated him. Dimitri was a sophomore at UPenn, a physics major, sort of a nerd, sort of a geek, who had taken up surfing and dragged Jimmy along in his wake.

Jimmy was a junior at Upper Cape Cod Regional Technical high school. He was not a physics major. He was an athlete, a three-sport starter in lacrosse, soccer, and wrestling. And a surfer. A darn good surfer.

"Okay, okay," Jimmy mumbled under his breath.

He shoved through the water for three steps, then sprung smoothly into a prone position on the board. The cold Atlantic sucked into his wet suit and made it hard to catch his breath. He felt his body shrink away from the cold, and to combat it, he paddled as hard as he could. He could not get warm. He spotted one of the gulls from earlier sitting on the water. The gull stared back at him with a sharp, appraising eye.

He paddled fifty yards out. Half a football field. The swells coming at him only bubbled up three feet or so, then ran forward and crashed on the sandy beach of Wellfleet. Not great surf. Nothing special. Jimmy had tried to tell Dimitri that they could wait and have better sets later in the week when the weather people forecasted a storm, but Dimitri wouldn't hear it. He wanted to surf. So Jimmy went with him.

"You realize we're the only ones out here, right?" Jimmy said to Dimitri when he paddled up beside him. More than anything else about surfing, Jimmy liked sitting next to his brother and talking.

"So what? We have the place to ourselves."

"That's because the waves suck, and it's freezing."

"You surf when you can, my young friend. Learn from your older brother."

Dimitri smiled. He always smiled. He had, Jimmy knew, a sunny disposition. And that could get irritating sometimes.

"Do you know you look ridiculous in your wet suit?" Jimmy asked.

Because he did. Dimitri looked like a cheerful black frog.

"I am one with the sea," Dimitri said. Then he lay down on his board and began paddling hard. "Here comes one."

Jimmy watched him. It was strange to be beyond the break. Jimmy always found it strange. Watching from out beyond the break, anyone paddling for a wave disappeared temporarily, then rose up, and suddenly appeared, gliding along the water's surface. Pretty remarkable, really. Jimmy watched Dimitri until his brother fell off the wave. Then he was alone.

He looked out at the horizon. Far out, misty in the morning fog, he saw a tanker sliding by on its way south. A few clouds tucked close to the horizon, blending with the sea. He could not hear a thing this far out except the gentle wash of the water when it rubbed against the sand of the beach. He smiled.

Dimitri had been right to get him out of bed on such a morning.

He shook himself. His sleepiness gave way to attention. He could surf. He was a good surfer. That's what he told himself. When it came to bats, balls, and balance, he had skills. Mad skills. He counted three swells, all too puny to try for, but then he saw a good one rolling toward him. It built and piled on itself until he could sense the water's forward momentum.

"Okay," he whispered.

Sometimes he whispered to himself. He always had. It steadied him.

He stretched out on the board and dug his hands into the water. He maneuvered his board into position, paddling until he was an arrow on the bowstring of the wave. Now, at last, he felt somewhat warmer. He felt his pecs stretch with the burden of paddling. He kicked softly with his feet, using them as rudders, his breath coming in short, quick pants. Although Dimitri meant it as a joke, Jimmy *did* feel one with the sea. Ridiculous, he told himself. He was turning into a nerd like his brother.

Then something hard and as explosive as Thor's hammer hit him from below.

He flew into the air.

Three feet up, and when he came down, his legs dunked into the water while he grabbed for the board with his arms.

What the . . . , he thought.

If what he felt could be called thought.

He looked around, scared suddenly, and tried to climb back onto the board. In the next instant, however, something fierce and horrible grabbed his leg. A pain more terrifying, more excruciating, than anything he had ever experienced ran like a million hornet stings into his brain. He screamed. It came from way, way down. It filled every molecule of his brain and body.

He tried to yank his leg away, but he had nothing to grasp except the board. The board flipped over. It skittered across the surface of the water and then jerked to a stop against the tether. The pain kept ringing and ringing and ringing in every cell.

Something violet and red began spreading around him. A few gulls ducked down and circled close. And then he saw a huge black fin cut the water next to him.

"Shark!" he screamed.

Because what else do you call? he wondered.

That part of his brain still worked and still laughed at his predicament. He yanked the tether cord toward him, and the board came back into reach. He flipped it fast and tried to pull himself up on it, but the fin suddenly wiggled next to him and he realized—*oh no, oh no, oh no*—that the animal attached to the fin was on him.

"Shark!" he shouted again, but this time his voice didn't work.

Then in one quick jerk, he went below water, his hands slipping off the board and saying goodbye to it. He looked at the shark and saw it. *Saw it!* It was huge and dark and its eye looked at him impassively, almost curious, and for an instant, he felt no fear. None. He decided he could go now, he could go with the shark, they could swim off into the gray-green water and live happily ever after.

And then—as much in dull wonder as anything

else—he reached forward and tried to poke the shark in the eye. That much he remembered. You should try to poke a shark in the eye if it grabbed you. So he did. He did not expect it to work, but to his amazement, the shark immediately released him and swam away, its fin cutting little slits in the sunlight above them both.

Jimmy turned and grabbed the tether, and he pulled himself up onto the surfboard. He did not look down, and he did not look at his leg.

What leg? his mind asked.

His leg looked like a mangled hunk of ham. Like shark leftovers, left in the fridge for a midnight snack.

Dimitri suddenly appeared next to him.

"Jimmy? Jimmy?" Dimitri kept asking.

"Get me to shore," Jimmy whispered. "A shark . . ."

"You're bleeding. Oh no, you're bleeding."

"Get me to shore. My leg—"

The fin appeared again, this time in front of both boards. Dimitri screamed at it. But the shark disappeared below, and Jimmy paddled forward, his hands still working, the sea still lifting him like a plate being put on a shelf.

Massachusetts.

Barn Whimbril looked at the word backward and forward, up and down, but he couldn't quite get his mind to wrap around it.

He had spent years thinking about Massachusetts. About the Red Sox. About his dad, who spent summers in Massachusetts. But he had never thought seriously about visiting Massachusetts until two weeks before, when his mother, Jane Whimbril, had dropped it into their conversation like someone dropping a sugar cube into a cup of tea.

A friend of mine has invited us to visit her on Cape Cod, his mom had said. *Cape Cod, Massachusetts. You remember her, I bet. Gail Polland. She's a famous writer.*

And? he asked, because he knew she had mentioned it for a reason.

And I thought maybe I'd say yes. That we would say yes. You'll be finished with school by then.

That's how he found himself sitting on a plane bound for Boston. That's how he found himself looking at the in-flight computer screen tracking across the Eastern Seaboard. Sarasota to Logan airport. Three and a half hours.

Florida to Massachusetts.

"Are you hungry, Barn? I've got those dried dates you like. And I packed us some carrot sticks. And we have power bars."

"I'm okay, Mom, thanks."

His mom slipped her arm through his. She liked it when they could sit quietly and talk, and a plane was as good a place as any for that, he guessed. He liked having his mom's arm under his. She smelled like lemongrass. She always did. She wore an oatmeal-colored sweater, a long paisley skirt, and Birkenstocks on her feet. Kind of a hippie, Barn understood. His mom taught English at Sarasota High School back home in Florida.

"You excited?" she asked.

"I guess so."

"Gail is an old friend. She's done very well for herself. We went to high school together. I remember her always writing. Always. Diaries, little books, projects, you name it. We grew up side by side. It would be like you visiting your buddy Finn twenty years from now."

Barn nodded. His mom had already told him about Gail, and she had made the comparison to Finn a half dozen times. It was almost as if she had to offer a reason for visiting an old friend. He had googled Gail Polland and checked her out. It was true: She was a famous writer. If he understood it correctly, she wrote mysteries set in England in the early 1900s. In her pictures, she looked older than his mom. She wore a lot of scarves.

He had also googled Woods Hole. Jessup Sabine, his friend and supervisor at the Florida Fish and Game, had informed him that Woods Hole, Massachusetts, was one of the top ocean research facilities on the Eastern Seaboard. Barn had plans to visit it midweek of their stay. Jessup used to work out of Woods Hole, and if he could get a break from work down in Florida, he planned to join them. That was still up in the air.

"Dad worked on Cape Cod, right?" Barn asked a few minutes later. He already knew the answer, but he liked hearing the stories anyway.

"Yes, out in Provincetown. At the end of the Cape. He did beach cleanup. Mostly custodial stuff. He was young. He always loved talking about that summer."

"And he lived on a boat?"

"For one summer he did. The *Dog Bite*. It was a funny boat. A man rented it to him. It was just set up on braces at the side of his house. In summer, Cape Cod gets tremendously crowded so people can rent out almost anything for top dollars."

"And everyone up here is a Red Sox fan like dad was?"

She squeezed his arm. He could never tell if she hurt when she talked about his dad, her husband, who had died in Afghanistan. He guessed it was a little hurt and a little love mixed together. Barn thought about his dad often. He couldn't help asking questions sometimes.

"Pretty much, honey. Be careful not to say anything nice about the Yankees. It's the best rivalry in sports. That's what your dad always told me."

"I won't. Go, Sox. Yankees suck."

"Maybe we can get you to a game at Fenway. Gail knows people. She's not exactly a sports person, so I don't know. Maybe we'll just enjoy the beach."

"Anything would be great, Mom. We can play it by ear."

Then something happened that often happened to him. One of the flight attendants stopped in the aisle beside him and smiled. She was a woman about his mom's age, maybe late thirties, who had a helmet of blond hair and a lot of makeup. She wore blue rubber gloves and carried a small plastic bag for picking up glasses and snack wrappings.

"Can I just say," she said, bending over slightly so that she made them into a cozy conversational triangle, "that your son has incredible hair?"

Barn felt himself blushing. People often commented on

his red hair. He always thought his red hair made him look like a rooster, a Rhode Island Red. It drove him nuts.

"It's gorgeous, isn't it?" his mom said, leaning across him as if she had to whisper with the flight attendant. "It's the perfect shade of red."

"Thanks," Barn said, because he found saying thanks got him out of most predicaments.

Red like a chicken, Barn thought. *Like a Rhode Island Red rooster.*

The flight attendant stood and crinkled the bag in her hand as if to say she had to get back to work. Then she smiled hard and headed down the aisle.

"Are you sure you don't want a snack?" his mom asked.

Before he could answer, his phone began playing the theme song from *Jaws*.

Duh duh. Dun duh dun duh dun duh, faster and faster.

It was a ringtone from the international shark file. And it meant only one thing:

Fatal shark attack.

2

Barn opened the message and turned his body so that the light from above the seat did not obscure the screen. He took a deep breath. He reminded himself, as he always did before reading the events of a shark attack, that the tragedy was authentic. It was not made up. Someone had been in the water, had felt the terror of an attack, had fought for her or his life against a creature much better adapted for swimming. It was no joke. He never wanted to lose sight of that. He had been in the water with sharks once himself. It could still make him shake to remember it. Sometimes he woke from bad dreams, shark dreams, and it took a long time to fall back asleep afterward.

Letting his breath out, he read:

Activity: Morning surf outing.

Case: GSAF 2021 10–832

Date: June 11, 2021

Location: The incident took place at Wellfleet Beach, Cape Cod, Massachusetts, USA

Name of Victim: Jimmy Xanthopoulous

Description: 17–year–old male from Wellfleet, MA.

Background Weather: The air temperature at Wellfleet Beach was 57 degrees F. Local stations report cloudy skies with a dew point of 60 F, humidity 57%, sea level pressure 27.1, and a slight breeze (3 mph) from the north.

Moon Phase: Three–quarter waxing moon.

Sea Conditions: Mean low tide occurred at 05h24, mean high tide at 12h04.

Distance from Shore: 50+ yards.

Depth of water: 30 feet approx.

Time: 8:30 a.m.

Narrative: A morning surfing trip with his older brother, Dimitri. Boys' father owns local pizza shop. Surviving brother reports the shark hit the board from underneath, knocking the victim off his surfboard. Shark then closed on the victim, administering fatal bite. The victim was an athlete, and it was likely his conditioning kept him alive and conscious as long as it did. He was able to speak when he was carried onto the beach and also when he was placed in the ambulance. He reported that the shark hit him solidly from below and then mauled him.

Injuries: Massive. Concentration of wounds on upper torso and leg. Fatal. Died on way to the hospital.

First Aid: Medical attention received. Wellfleet EMT unit.

Species: According to witness, the shark presented itself in front of the surfboards after the attack. The assisting brother said

the shark had a large black dorsal fin and
trailed them into the surf. It did not rejoin
the attack. From the manner of the attack and
the size of the dorsal fin, a great white shark
is the probable predator.

Case Investigator: Chloe Jordan, GSAF

He read it three times. Each time he absorbed something new.

"Everything okay?" his mother asked, bumping him a
little with her shoulder.

"A shark attack. Actually, it happened near where we
will be staying, I think. Wellfleet, Mass. Is Gail's house
close to that?"

"It's in Wellfleet, actually. Right on the beach. What
was it?"

"Attack on a surfer."

"Fatal?"

He nodded.

"Oh dear," she said.

She held her hand out for his phone. He gave it to her.

She read the report from the Global Shark Attack File. Her face closed down in concentration. She passed the phone back to him when she finished.

"Terrible. Think of the family. And his brother was with him?"

"Yes. Seems that way."

"What do you think happened?"

Barn shrugged. He had already come up with a likely scenario. It was basic.

"The shark probably mistook him for a seal. I've read about the situation up here along the East Coast. The seal colonies have made a comeback, which is important environmentally, but great whites will follow the seals. If you put a person on a surfboard, especially in poor visibility, the shark looks up and sees what it thinks is a seal silhouette. So it comes up and thinks it's biting a seal, but it's a surfboard instead. If it causes the human to bleed in that first bite, well, then it has motive to keep coming. It's all a mistake but a deadly one."

"Oh dear, that's horrible. The poor family. I can't imagine what they are going through."

Barn nodded. It *was* horrible. He had read any number of accounts of great whites hitting at or striking at surfers. While it wasn't common, it also wasn't entirely rare. In fact, in South Africa and California, shark tours used to tow surfboards behind them, trying to get a great white to breach for the tourists. That practice had eventually been outlawed, but it had been effective. The tourists loved it, but it was dangerous for the sharks and a bad idea to train them to hit surfboards. It was unnatural and stupid when you came right down to it.

The great white presence was fairly new to the East Coast. To Massachusetts. Great whites had always lived in the waters off the East Coast, but the population had surged once seals had made a comeback. It was in the news a lot. At least it was in the shark news that people like Barn followed. In Chatham, in the center of the Cape, they played *Jaws* every night at a local theater throughout the summer.

Before he could say anything else to his mom, two texts came in. The first one was from Lucas Iglesias, owner and operator of AQUATARIUM, the best aquarium shop near

Barn's home in Sarasota. Lucas had the same feed from the Global Shark Attack File on his phone that Barn used.

L U see it?

Saw it. GWS.

L Great white shark.

Absolutely. It's the right predatory profile.

Then Margaret Valley wrote. She was the smartest girl in his class. And his friend. And the one girl he knew who made him tongue-tied and nervous and happy all at once.

M Check the Shark Attack file.

Saw it. GWS.

M So sad.

It's right where I will be.

M I might be up there too. TMTT

Too much to type.

Awesome!

 Long story. But yes.

He felt his face flush reading her message. Being around
her was like eating ice cream too fast. He wrote back.

Cool. We're going to be in Wellfleet.

I'll let you know.

Something about the plane's position canceled the last
message. At least he thought so. He put his phone down on
his lap. A bell rang and an announcement told him to turn
off electronic devices in preparation for landing. His
mother took his hand and squeezed it. She didn't love flying. She especially hated landings. He squeezed her hand
back. Boston Harbor appeared like a blue patch of sky
below him.

The Cape Cod traffic was intense. *Intense!*

Barn sat in the economy hatchback his mother had rented at Boston's Logan airport, his phone locked to Google Maps, his body sweltering in the heat. The car *did* have air-conditioning, but it barely worked, and he had already argued with his mother about whether having the windows up or down made more sense.

They had agreed on half-down with the air-conditioning at full blast.

It still didn't work.

"This—" he said, and she cut him off.

"I know, I know, I know. It's not great. Traffic is always like this heading toward the bridge. But it doesn't do us any good to get upset about it."

"What's the name of the bridge again?"

Barn thumbed through the map on his phone. Twice it had reported "traffic ahead."

"You're the navigator," she said. "You're the one with the phone. It goes over Buzzards Bay. Or no. It goes over the canal, I think."

Barn didn't mind having a mini project. He loved maps. He scrolled eastward until he saw the name: Sagamore Bridge. It stretched across the Cape Cod Canal. It connected the Massachusetts mainland to Route 6, the main highway down the center of the Cape. Barn jumped to a second screen he had been studying. It was the Cape Cod wiki page, and it gave information about the history of the Wampanoag Indians who had lived on the Cape for centuries, the arrival of the Pilgrims in 1620, and a few details about the kettle ponds formed by the retreat of the Laurentide ice sheet in the late Pleistocene era.

Barn knew that great whites had been swimming in the

waters around the Cape for 350 million years. Human history on the Cape was nothing compared to that. And just today, a shark and a human had collided.

"Can I get over to the right? Does he see me? Is he letting me change lanes?" his mom asked.

Barn looked at the car next to them. The driver was a heavy guy in a white T-shirt and a yellow construction hat. Barn tried to catch the guy's eye, but the guy ignored him.

"Not yet. The guy is staring straight ahead."

Then, wonders of wonders, the traffic finally began to move, and Barn helped guide his mom into the correct lane for the bridge. She was able to hit the gas and get them moving. It felt better. Air came into the car. Even the air-conditioning seemed to respond by throwing out a little frosty air.

It took five minutes to work through traffic to the main branch of Route 6. His mom looked in the rearview mirror constantly to gauge her place in traffic.

"When you go east, you're going 'down Cape,'" she said, leveling out the car at about fifty miles per hour, her eyes busy. "Coming back to the mainland is called going 'up Cape.'"

"How come?"

She shrugged.

"It just is," she said. "It's one of those things."

"Wouldn't it make more sense if you said 'up Cape' when you were going to the tip of Cape Cod?"

"Take it up with the locals, Barn. I'm just a tourist."

Barn looked out the window. At last it started to feel like a beachy place. He saw sand on the roadside and some scrubby-looking pines. Also, the light changed. When he looked to the distance, he could tell that a few miles away the land gave up. The sea took over then. Gulls glided in the sky, and the breeze that came through their windows smelled of salt and seaweed. It always made him feel better to be next to the ocean. He supposed most people felt better when they stood on a beach looking out at the water. Something old about it. Something primitive. He didn't know what it was, but he knew it existed.

When he looked back at his mom, he saw tears in her eyes. He hadn't expected that.

"Are you okay, Mom?"

"I'm fine, honey."

"But you're . . ."

She nodded and rubbed the heel of her hand against her eyes.

"Your dad and I dated here a long, long time ago. It's just bringing back memories."

"I'm sorry, Mom."

"Oh, don't be sorry. These are good tears, darling. These are tears of memory. If you're lucky, tears of memory should always be happy."

But his dad was gone. Killed in Afghanistan. Nothing happy about that.

He reached over and took her hand.

"I'm glad we came up here, Mom."

"Are you?" she said, and turned and smiled.

It broke his heart to see tears in her eyes.

"I am, Mom. I like knowing you two dated here a long time ago."

She smiled. Then she rubbed her hand against her eyes again. She took a deep breath, then changed the subject.

"Did Margaret and Finn figure out if they could come to the Cape on their trip?"

"Would they be going down Cape or up Cape, Mom?"

She let go of his hand and playfully slapped his knee. He smiled and rolled his window a little lower.

"They'll make it out, I think. I hope so. It depends on a few things, but they should be able to make it."

"Good. You'll have some company beside two old ladies catching up on things you know nothing about."

"And Jessup will be up?"

"I think he said he would. He's attending a conference."

Barn nodded slowly. He wanted to see Jessup, but it surprised him when his mom seemed to know more about Jessup than Barn did himself.

He wanted to ask about it, but then they finally broke into a free span on the highway, and his mom turned on the radio. She found some classical music, looked at him, raised her eyebrows, then nodded. He nodded back. It was okay with him. She loved classical music.

It took two hours to make it to Wellfleet. When they finally entered the beach area, his mom started leaning forward and looking back and forth, trying to pick up landmarks.

"She said to look for a gray house . . . weathered cedar shingles. With white porch posts. I've seen pictures—it's a beautiful . . . What's the number on that house? Your eyes are better than mine, Barn."

"Seventy-two."

"She's at eighty-eight. Are we going in the right direction?"

"We're here pretty much, Mom. The phone says we reached our destination."

And then they did. Barn saw the house. It was unmistakable, really. It was large and handsome with a wide porch that wrapped around three-quarters of the building's skirting. It was precisely as his mother had described it. The beach stretched out across the road.

"Oh, how lovely!" his mom said.

"It's great, Mom."

"Oh, how lovely," she said again.

Barn had a moment then of seeing his mom. Of seeing her as she might have been as a young girl. Or as a young woman meeting his dad for the first time. He felt a little teary himself watching her. He had lost his dad, true, but she had lost her husband, her friend, her partner, and an entire history that she could never replace. Her friend Gail could remember some of that history with her. Barn sensed that's why she had wanted so much to come to Cape Cod.

"We're here!" she said once she had pulled in the sandy driveway and turned off the engine. "I can hardly believe it. Oh, Barn, smell the sea. How lucky are we? How lucky are we to have this day?"

Barn agreed. But as he climbed out of the car, watching as Gail Polland came out of the door and made a sweet, happy sound accompanied by a vigorous wave, he was aware that just behind, just out beyond the breakers, a fellow on a surfboard had met one of the oldest residents of Cape Cod: the great white.

An hour later, after saying hello, getting shown to a guest room, letting Gail examine him closely and comment about his resemblance to various family members—"But where did that glorious red hair come from?" she asked— Barn stood on the sand and studied the water. He had been itching to get to the beach as soon as he had heard about the attack. He took a deep breath. He smelled the ocean. The water was gray and flat and even. A mist touched the surface of the sea and ran in a soft blue haze all the way to the horizon. A few gulls made quiet calls behind him, roaming the beach searching for food left behind by the steady stream of beachgoers that usually visited Wellfleet Beach.

But not today. Few visitors walked the beach and no swimmers. The weather had kept them away, Barn figured, but so had the shark attack. The whole place had an empty feeling, like a gym after a game. Something had gone on, an event had occurred, but now it was over, and the place felt hollow.

He took a dozen photos of the surf and the water. The sound of his phone camera clicking carried in the damp air. As he finished, he looked up to see a pickup truck rolling slowly along the beach toward him. The truck kept to the hard-packed sand well away from the high tide mark. He didn't expect to see a vehicle on a beach, but looking closely he saw it belonged to the Town of Wellfleet. He smelled gasoline burning and the exhaust discharge.

A teenage boy jumped out of the truck when it came to a stop and grabbed a sign and a two-pound sledgehammer from the truck bed. The driver of the truck, an older, scruffy guy wearing a blue bandana on his head, instructed the kid how to hammer in the stake.

"Make sure you get it in about two feet," the older man said, "and make sure you do it straight. Do it right."

"Yes, Frankie," the teenager called back, obviously only half listening to the older man.

"I mean it, Caleb. Do it right."

Barn walked over and took a picture of the sign in the kid's hand. He wanted to send it to Lucas and Margaret and Finn.

The sign had a circle with a red line through a stick figure of a person swimming. Below the person swimming was the word SHARK. A picture of a helicopter hovered above the person swimming.

"Did it happen near here?" Barn asked the kid.

"Over there," the kid said, pointing with his chin to the area of water maybe an eighth of a mile to the east.

"And he was surfing, right?"

The kid didn't answer. He was having trouble holding the sign and hitting it with the sledge at the same time. Barn put his phone in the pocket of his windbreaker and knelt down to hold the sign steady for the kid.

"Thanks," the kid said.

"Don't hit the boy and kill him," the older guy in the truck called over. "We'll be sued back to the Stone Age."

"You could get out and help, you know? How would that be, Frankie? Wouldn't that be some kind of miracle?"

The kid smiled at Barn.

"Lazzzzzzzyyyyyy," he whispered.

The kid—Caleb—hammered the top of the stake until the bottom held steady in the sand. Barn stepped back so the kid could swing the sledge more freely. It only took three swings to get the sign fixed properly.

"Hey, brain boy," Frankie called, "you need to turn the sign around. You have it facing out to the water. Do you expect the sharks to read it?"

Barn saw that Frankie had a point. Caleb bent over and yanked the stake out. He turned it around so that it faced the beach parking lot. Barn held the sign again to help out. This time the sign went in with a lean to the left, but Caleb straightened it by tapping it with the hammer.

"Did you know the victim?" Barn asked.

"No, didn't know him. I guess he was local, though."

"Did they catch the shark?"

Caleb leaned on the stake. He was a chubby kid with wild hair that blew every which way in the wind.

"I don't think so. They've had boats and copters out looking. That shark could be miles away by now. People have been out fishing for sharks, but they've only brought in a few. The whole Cape has gone nuts about great whites. You can't really blame people. A kid died. It's a huge deal."

"How long will the beach be closed?"

"I don't know. I've heard different estimates. I mean, it's just like *Jaws*. That's what everyone is saying. I mean, that story took place on Cape Cod. It's just like this. Killer shark, you know. Out to get everyone. But you know, this is a tourist destination, too. So people are going back and forth about whether to close the beach, for how long, all that. Money is the bottom line around here."

"Actually, I think *Jaws* was set in Martha's Vineyard, but that's pretty weird no matter what. Do you know what they did with the surfboard?"

"The kid's surfboard? Heck, I don't know. Hey, Frankie, do you know what they did with the kid's surfboard?"

Frankie shook his head. Then he told Caleb to get back

in so they could finish putting up the rest of the signs. Frankie had his phone out, typing.

"Thanks," Barn said. "Thanks for filling me in."

"Lot of surfers these days. I mean, a lot of people are out in the water. Wind surfers go way out," Caleb said. "People are betting there will be another attack."

"It's pretty rare," Barn said. "Crocodiles on the Nile kill around a thousand people a year. Sharks only kill maybe fifty people around the world."

"Crocodiles on the Nile?" Frankie asked as Caleb shut the door and tossed the sledge on the dashboard. "What kind of freak knows how many people are killed by crocodiles on the Nile? Give me a break, kid."

"I think it's cool to know that stuff," Caleb said. "Don't listen to Frankie. He's old and crabby. And he's a Yankee fan. It's disgusting. No one on Cape Cod likes him."

Frankie shook his head and put the truck in gear. Caleb fist bumped with Barn as the truck pulled away. Barn smiled and went back to study the water some more. He saw a fisherman about a quarter of a mile south along the line of surf. He walked down to talk to him.

The fisherman was a tall, skinny guy with a hat that had a long brim. The brim made him resemble a bird ready to peck forward. Barn approached slowly. Sometimes fishermen were friendly, and sometimes they were grumpy. Some came out to be social, and some came out to be alone. Barn couldn't tell what sort this guy was.

"Having any luck?" Barn asked.

Barn kept his distance. He didn't want to crowd the guy.

"I'm alive and breathing," the man said, staring straight to sea. "That's pretty lucky. Any day you're alive and breathing, that's lucky."

Barn nodded.

"I guess I mean with fishing."

"A couple dogfish. I released them."

"What do you get mostly?"

The man sat on a stool beside his three casting rods. Everything about him pointed to the sea. Barn could imagine the fish grabbing the line and yanking him into the water with them.

"Usual stuff. Porgies. Dogfish. Sometimes blues."

"Anybody fishing for the white sharks?"

The man swiveled his head to regard Barn. Barn tried to imagine how this guy ever left the beach. Everything about him seemed salty. He was pretty old, and his legs were thin.

"Some idiots came down here with a rowboat and some dead woodchucks. I kid you not. They rowed out and hung the woodchucks on lines, you know, with a float tied to them. No law against it, I guess. I don't know what they expected."

"Did they get anything?"

The man looked at Barn as if Barn had asked the goofiest question ever.

"No, they didn't get anything. Who in the world ever heard of using woodchucks for bait?"

"Sorry."

The man sighed. He stood and stretched his back, then sat again. He put one finger against the line on his first pole and flexed the line a little. Somewhere out in the waves, Barn guessed, the bait he used fluttered.

"Woodchucks for great whites. I mean. People get stupid ideas when a shark takes a bite out of someone. They closed the beach here and I don't blame them, but people don't have to be in a panic about it. Sharks coming to hunt seals, is all. It's the natural way of things. Of course, it's more real than just about anything you can imagine. Shark attack is a horrible way to go."

Barn nodded. He knew what the fisherman said was correct. He knew from his own experience. He knew it in his night terrors when he woke and felt like something round and deadly had just swum beneath him.

"The seals ever go after your bait?"

"Not mine. A friend of mine had a seal take his whole rig. Before he could reach down and grab his pole, the seal had the thing dragging across the sand. Impressive, I'll tell you. A seal is a big animal. Ask any surfer. Seals can come around and make their lives miserable."

"Well, thanks," Barn said.

"Where you from, anyway?"

"Florida."

"Whereabouts?"

"Sarasota."

The man nodded. Barn never knew why one person

asked another where she or he was from, then nodded as if it confirmed something once they got the answer.

"Come winter, that's where I should be. Down on a beach in Sarasota."

"Thanks," Barn said again.

The man reached forward and strummed the fishing line closest to him. The line ran all the way out beyond the breakers. The man nodded as if he had struck the right note.

The great white shark swam twenty-seven feet below the surface and fifteen feet above the ocean bottom. A female, 12.6 feet long, with bright black eyes and a mouth that grinned if seen from the proper angle. Called a white pointer in Australia, or white death in other countries, the female shark had already lived twenty-three of its projected life span of seventy years. It weighed 2,700 pounds and could swim, when closing on prey, up to thirty-five miles per hour. Due to its coloring—gray on top, white below—the shark blended well with the dark water. An ambush predator, it made its kills by streaking up from below.

Like all great white sharks, this one swimming off Wellfleet was an apex predator. The only creatures able to prey on it were orcas and humans.

It swam unobserved despite the helicopter that sometimes patrolled nearby. The boats that swarmed over the area had missed it. It swam leisurely, sometimes opening its mouth to increase the oxygen flow over its gills. It had eaten a gray seal six hours before, exactly at dawn, so it did not feel particularly hungry. At the same time, it tracked its environment for possible prey. It would not turn away from food if it came across it.

Five hundred feet off Nauset Beach, it sensed an electric charge in the water and heard noises that made it curious. At first neither the charge nor the noise meant anything. Then the noise grew louder. Instinctively it turned its head in the direction of the noise and the electric pulse strengthened. Prey animals gave off electric charges and often made splashing noises, so both messages coming to its senses suggested it was worthwhile to investigate.

Moving with more purpose, it swam directly perpendicular to the beach, moving calmly out to sea. In an eighth of a mile, it saw the boat. It swam well beneath the flat bottom of the vessel, then circled and rose up the water column until it felt comfortable rising partially out of the water.

The shark sensed movement above the water. But it had no concept of boat, nor did it understand that what it saw walking on the deck was a man. Moreover, it didn't care. Of all sharks, the great white was the only species believed to be capable of seeing prey on land. It had gained the ability to see seals resting on rocks. Now it regarded the boat, saw nothing compelling in its appraisal, then slowly sank back into the depths. It circled gradually toward the shoreline, where the seal pups would be learning to swim and slide off rocks.

Gail Polland had a small heater going on the porch.

It was a gas heater, hooked into the wall, made to resemble a fireplace. Gail and Barn's mother sat at a table directly in front of the gas fireplace, a deluxe Scrabble board spread out on a table before them. They both held large mugs of tea. His mother could beat just about anyone in Scrabble, but Barn wondered, as he climbed the steps to the wide porch of the house overlooking the beach, how she would fare against a world-famous writer.

"Your mother is a devastating Scrabble player," Gail said when he climbed the last step and stood at their level.

"You should have told me, Barn. And she's so fast! I no sooner lay down a word then she comes right back with a bigger and better one that fits in just so . . ."

Barn nodded. It was nice on the porch. The whole house was nice. Amazing, even.

"How did it go?" his mom asked, her eyes down on the board. She moved the Scrabble tiles in various ways in her wooden tray, lining them up to try different words.

"They closed the beach," Barn said.

"I heard they might," Gail said, then sipped her tea. "I guess it's better safe than sorry, but they can't truly do anything about it, can they, Barn?"

Barn shrugged and pulled up a seat between the two women.

"I guess they could hope it would leave," Barn said, "but that's not likely. It has all the conditions it needs. Food, good water temperatures, all that. It might even be here to mate, although I doubt that. No one has ever seen great whites mating. Not once."

"Really?" Gail asked. "With all the cameras and nature programs . . . not once? I find that extraordinary. And refreshing. Good for them. They should have a little privacy."

Barn smiled. He liked Gail. She was funny.

Barn could tell his mom was loving the visit. Her shoulders had relaxed, and she looked hazy and sleepy.

"Some scientists speculate that the western great whites congregate in winter off of Mexico," Barn said, not sure if he was talking too much about sharks. But he had to finish. "The thinking is they mate there. I don't think they're sure about the Atlantic great white sharks."

"Here's something I've always wondered," Gail said, putting her cup on the table. "Why 'great white shark'? I mean, are their minor white sharks? Why 'great'?"

"Or 'pretty good white sharks'?" his mom asked, getting into it. "Fair question, Gail."

"I don't honestly know," Barn said.

"I know there are great blue herons," Gail said. "But I don't think there are 'fairly good blue herons.'"

"It's a good question. I'll have to research it," Barn said.

"I once had a writing teacher who said every story

should be an answer to a question," Gail said. "She said if you don't discover what the question is, then you don't know what you're writing about. So maybe that's a little seed for us to think about."

"I love that," his mom said. "I'm going to use it in my classes. And maybe we need to discover why it's 'great white shark' and not 'merely okay white shark.'"

Before anyone could say anything else, or make a play, a car pulled into the driveway.

Then a strange thing happened.

He watched as Gail and his mom exchanged a look.

Their eyes moved quickly into each other's gaze, and then Barn watched his mother blush. A moment later, he understood why.

Jessup Sabine, part of the Florida Fish and Game, a man who wore a ten-inch machete on his leg, slid out of the driver's side door and smiled at them all.

"This must be the place," he said with the world's slowest Southern drawl. "Didn't even take a wrong turn."

Barn watched Jessup come up the steps. Watching him, Barn experienced a small mental dislocation. Jessup

Sabine belonged to the Florida swamps, to alligators and long-legged birds, to coral snakes and pink-eyed possums.

He did not belong in Massachusetts. Or Cape Cod.

Seeing him here was like watching a polar bear stroll down a street in New York City. It didn't compute. He was a tall, big man, maybe six foot three, with an enormous moustache and happy blue eyes. The moustache made it look like he had parked a horse somewhere. He had light brown hair, gray around the edges, and thick shoulders. His left arm from the elbow down was gone, and in its place was a metal-and-plastic prosthetic. His keys jingled in his pocket. He wore a green Fish and Game shirt with his name in threads across the pocket: JESSUP SABINE.

If Jessup felt out of place, he didn't give any sign of it. Neither did Barn's mother. She stood and smiled and walked to meet Jessup as he cleared the steps.

"Jessup, I'd like you to meet my friend Gail. Gail, this is Jessup."

Barn watched, wondering what exactly Jessup meant to his mother. Or, for that matter, what his mother meant to

Jessup. It wasn't quite clear, though Barn guessed they liked each other in a romantic way. Meanwhile, Jessup stepped across the porch and shook hands with Gail. Gail invited him to sit. Jessup pulled over another chair and squeezed in beside Barn.

"How you doing, Barn?" Jessup asked, his words dropping one by one out of his mouth, his attitude as casual about things as it always was. "How do you like Massachusetts?"

"I like it fine," Barn answered. "Glad you could make it up here."

"I had time in between sessions at my conference. Your mom invited me to stop by, and I took her up on it. I worked up here years ago. Nice to be back. Nice to have some summer weather."

Barn watched his mother's eyes pass to Jessup's, then drop to her Scrabble tiles again. It might have been an awkward moment, except that Gail and Jessup seemed to be long-lost friends. Gail asked a dozen questions about the conference and then asked him about his work at the Florida Fish and Game.

"Oh, about a third conservation, a third law enforcement, and a third public relations," Jessup said. "It keeps us busy."

"Barn is an intern there," Barn's mom said. "Officially."

"That's right," Jessup said. "He's our shark expert."

"We've just been talking about the attack on the surfer," Gail said. "It's a dreadful situation. I keep thinking about that poor boy and his family. And now they've closed the beach."

"That's what I heard. People at the conference are talking about it. They've tagged quite a few sharks in the area. Pokey Bob said . . . Do you know him, Gail?"

"Pokey Bob? What a wonderful name. I don't know him, though."

"His real name is Bob Crescent. He has been tagging sharks so long that he got nicknamed Pokey. He's always poking something. It's a running gag."

His mother stayed quiet. Barn suspected it was out of nervousness. She seemed flustered now that Jessup had arrived.

"Anyway, Pokey Bob said they're seeing a sizeable

increase in white sharks. They're not sure why, although it's easy enough to piece together. Probably better food. Increased seal populations. It makes sense, of course. Increase the food, increase the predators."

"Tell me, do you think the boy who was killed . . . ? Did the shark know what it was doing?" Gail asked, sipping her tea.

"Depends what you mean by 'know what it's doing.' It knows how to hunt, that's for sure. From everything we know, though, most great white attacks on surfers are done from confusion. The shark isn't out to get a surfer. That would be a misunderstanding of the situation."

"I'd like to see the surfboard," Barn said. "We might be able to tell something by looking at it."

"Like what?" asked Gail.

"Oh, it's hard to say. You might be able to tell if the shark came from below, or if it bit the board in the surface slosh. If it came from below, it's probably deadlier. From the side, well, it might have been testing. It's like looking at a crime scene," Barn said.

Barn's mom asked Jessup if he would like a cup of tea.

"Thank you, but I can't stay. Actually, I came to borrow Barn, if I could. A few researchers are taking a ride out to where the attack took place. It would be a good opportunity for Barn to meet some shark folks."

"And Pokey Bob?" Gail asked.

"Not today. What do you say, Barn? Want to keep me company? I'll get you back a little after sunset."

Barn looked at his mom. His mom nodded and raised her eyebrows. The gesture meant he could go if he liked.

"Grab a jacket," she said. "Or a sweater. The sun doesn't seem to be coming out today."

Barn watched the seals. Seals and gulls. The water below
the boat, a thirty-two-foot converted fishing boat named
Silly Ray, glimmered gray and pale and deep. Great white
water, Barn couldn't help thinking. People thought of
sharks as living in southern climates, in tropical blue water,
and that was true, but great whites lived at least part of the
year in chilly waters. They lurked below, watching the surface for the necessary silhouette, then shot up in a great
openmouthed rush to wound the seal or sea bird or human
on a surfboard. They rolled their eyes backward before
impact, so when they bit, they were effectively blind.

You would never know a great white swam below you until you found yourself in its mouth. That's what Barn thought.

"Can't tell a whole heck of a lot," Dr. Fitzgibbon said beside him, her eyes studying the same scene as Barn. "It's pretty much what you would expect. Seals and rocks. I imagine the whites patrol wherever the first drop off to deeper ocean occurs."

Barn glanced over at Dr. Fitzgibbon. He still could not believe he stood beside arguably the greatest living expert on great whites. She was a professor at Stanford, although she spent her summers at Woods Hole, Massachusetts. She was tall and slim, like a seahorse balanced carefully in quiet water. But what Barn liked best about her was her refusal to condescend to him. It was an honor to be next to her.

"What do you see, Barn?" she asked after they had watched a little longer. "I'm interested in your observations."

"It's a classic scene. The whole situation is perfect for the whites to ambush the seals. I've read about this sort of thing, but this is my first time seeing it. You couldn't draw it out any better."

"It's been going on thousands of years," Dr. Fitzgibbon said, her eyes scanning the water. "Longer than we know. Sharks cull the pod and keep it vital. It's like wolves eating caribou. It maintains balance in both populations."

"What brought the seals back?"

"Oh, a combination of things, I suppose. Better environmental standards. Better fishing practices. The coastal management agencies have placed moratoriums on certain ground stocks . . . cod especially. More fish, more seals. More seals, more sharks. Circle of life and all that."

The boat rolled up and down. Gulls called from the rocks. A bright breeze flicked at the water top, throwing foam and mist into the air when it picked up speed. Barn pinched his jacket closer to his neck. It was a raw day.

"Do you think there will be another attack?"

"It wouldn't surprise me either way. One thing we know. The sharks haven't changed. People changed. We are in the water more, doing water sports, surfing, scuba diving. You know all that, of course. The public, though, the public has a hard time understanding that a shark has no interest in harming you. It only wants to eat."

"Like everything on Earth."

Dr. Fitzgibbon smiled.

Then, in almost the same instant, she pointed at the rocks.

"There!" she said.

Barn saw it. It was a swirl, that was all, but there was no doubt a shark had just made a run at a seal. The seal shot off in a different direction, and the shark's dorsal fin disappeared almost at once. The water continued rocking, and three gulls, all heavy, mature birds, pushed off the water surface and began croaking their calls of alarm.

Then, amazingly, a second shark flew up through the air with the runaway seal in its mouth. The same seal that had just escaped. Barn heard people behind him yell with delight and fear. Everyone had seen it! It was like spotting a shooting star. The front quarter of the shark splashed down hard on the water, and the seal began paddling away, injured and bleeding.

Gulls swooped down, looking for pieces of seal.

"That was a second shark!" Dr. Fitzgibbon said, her voice edgy with excitement. "I've never seen it before . . . Oh, look, look!"

It was gruesome but fascinating. Barn couldn't look away. The shark that had managed to bite the seal now swam close to it. Barn felt the anticipation of the moment. *Now, now, now, now* and then boom, the shark tore into the crippled seal. The shark's full head came out of the water and then it began thrashing back and forth, ripping the seal meat, scattering bits of flesh on the surface of the sea.

"They might have been hunting in pairs," Dr. Fitzgibbon said, clearly moved and astonished. "I've read about the behavior, but I've never seen an example of it. I am not even sure it's been substantiated."

"Cooperative hunting," Barn said.

"You're good luck, Barn. Wow, that was something . . . Oh, there, the second one is circling out beyond a little ways. Do you see, Barn?"

Barn did see.

It was the most spectacular thing he had ever seen. It

was more than he could comprehend. He realized that he had been holding his breath, more or less, since the attack occurred. He let out a stream of air and told himself to breathe evenly.

"What power," Dr. Fitzgibbon marveled. "It never ceases to amaze me."

And then the carcass went under. Gone. Blood continued to stain the water, but the flesh and sharks had disappeared. It was astonishing. Seal, gone. Shark, gone. The sea rolled onward, gathering everything and dispersing it. Barn felt a shiver run up and down his body. He had been in the water with sharks. With bulls. But even they did not demonstrate the ruthlessness—the completeness—of a great white shark attack.

"I'd keep the beach closed," Dr. Fitzgibbon said when she turned to face him. "At least for a while. Wouldn't you, Barn?"

7

The next morning on Wellfleet Beach, Barn met up with his two closest friends.

He had come out to fly a kite, a present from Gail, and the stiff breeze blowing out to sea promised an easy launch. The weather still hadn't cleared. It was gray and cloudy, and now and then Barn felt rain spitting. The weather report called for more of the same. The BEACH CLOSED signs remained. His mom had made him promise not to enter the water.

She didn't need to make him promise. His experience

with bull sharks on Apple Way Canal was all the reminder he needed.

He had tied the string onto the kite, then let it go out a few feet. It was an airfoil-type kite that went up easily. He let it out a little farther, just to test it, and that was when he heard someone calling his name. He cocked his head, listening, then shrugged his shoulders. *Probably the gulls*, he figured. Gulls sounded a lot like humans calling when the voices got trapped in the wind.

"What are you doing, Barn?"

He turned in the other direction, toward the rocks where the young man had been killed, and he saw Margaret and Finn walking toward him.

Margaret Valley, he thought. It always made him a bit upside down to see her.

And Finn, his best friend, carried a backpack and his pair of shoes in his free hand.

"You're here!" Barn said, which was not the brightest thing he had ever said.

"Yes!" Margaret said.

An awkward thing happened then. He did a sort of

shoulder bump, pat-on-the-back type of hello with Finn. They always did that. That left the question, though, of how he was supposed to greet Margaret.

Hug?

No way.

Hand shake?

Ridiculous.

Shoulder bump, pat on the back?

He didn't think so.

Which left the question of what he *should* do. To his amazement, Margaret solved the problem for him. She stepped forward and hugged him. No big deal. Easy as that. Then she stepped back and smiled. In the same moment, his kite began to chatter and fluff in the increased wind.

"Cool kite," Finn said.

"How did you guys . . . ?" Barn asked.

"It's a long story," Margaret said, smiling and happy. She looked beautiful in the wind, her hair blowing so that she had to push it back from her face. "We're supposed to be up here looking at colleges. Not for me, but for my cousin, McCullough. She lives up here, and her mom is my mom's best friend. And they had a lot of marital trouble. McCullough's parents, I mean . . . anyway, there's no one to take McCullough on a college tour. So we're going to do that."

"And I came along because my parents are going on a trip to Mexico. It's like a second honeymoon or something. I'm staying with Margaret and her mom."

"So we're here. We're staying in the next town over. What's the name, Finn?"

"Mashpee."

Barn felt happy to have his friends with him. He would never have admitted it to his mom, but visiting with Gail was a little . . .

. . . slow.

Nothing wrong with it. Just a little tea and quiet and sleep. Maybe, though, it was the weather.

Either way, having his friends in Massachusetts with him was the best medicine. He told Finn to walk the kite away and toss it up when he said so. Finn threw down his backpack and trotted off, stopping now and then to let

Barn unspool the line. Margaret held her phone up and recorded the launch.

"Ready?" Barn called.

"Ready," Finn answered.

"Do it!"

Finn tossed the kite up. It shot up into the wind, took one wild, loopy dive, then began climbing like a rocket. Pretty soon the kite was a colorful speck in a gray sky.

"So was it right here?" Margaret asked.

Barn had to turn his attention away from the kite to see her expression.

She meant the shark. Was the shark attack here?

"Yes, a little to the east. There are some rocks over there, you can see them . . . and the seals are having their pups."

Margaret put the phone down by her side. She looked a long time at the water. Barn felt the kite tug at his hand, urging to go higher. Margaret wasn't joking or acting dramatic. He could tell she was touched by what had happened.

"That would be a terrible way to die," Margaret said.

"You'd be on your surfboard and looking for a ride and then suddenly it would all change. It would change in an instant. It's horrible."

"It was probably a mistake. A test bite. Once it smelled the blood, though, then it would have come back in again. It's what they do."

"So sad for his brother."

"Yes. Sad for everyone."

Finn came back, and Barn handed him the kite string. Margaret kept looking out at the water.

"We should put a GoPro on the kite," Finn said, excited.

Margaret suddenly turned and looked at them both.

"They're going in the water!" she said, pointing to the wash of water up the beach. "Surfers!"

Three surfers in wet suits carried their boards toward the waves. They didn't seem to be sneaking in or trying to hide. They walked with their boards under their arms, then pushed off into the breaking surf and started paddling toward the horizon. Barn watched them clear the first wave, then the second. They had the water to themselves. Climbing over the waves, the boards went nearly vertical, then slapped down on the far side. They paddled out until they could sit up on their boards and look back to land and out to sea. Eventually one of the surfers moved down onto his belly and began paddling and kicking. The wave lifted him, and for a moment, Barn couldn't be sure the surfer had succeeded in catching the curl. But then the wave grabbed the board and began running it forward— like someone shoving a shuffleboard disc—and the surfer popped to his feet and put his hands out on either side for balance. A classic stance.

The surfer bailed on his wave about halfway to the beach. By that time, a second surfer had caught a wave. He rode in a crouch, not as good as the first surfer, his arms moving in small circles to maintain balance. Someone yelled. The sound came from the third surfer, still sitting on his board, his hoots of encouragement rallying them to keep going, to keep surfing, to catch the best rides.

8

"They're teenagers!" Finn said.

Barn sat on a small rise of sand with his friends, watching the surfers. Finn slowly reeled the kite in by its string. Barn wasn't sure what he wanted to do about the surfers, or what *should* be done, but he understood it was a bad idea to be surfing.

Call the police?

That seemed extreme.

Yell at them to come back to shore?

He doubted they would listen. Besides, who was he? Policeman of the world? It wasn't his business.

"They're a little older than we are," Margaret said, squinting to see. "I think so, anyway. It's hard to see them clearly. And they have on wet suits."

"Are they in danger, Barn?" Finn asked.

"I mean . . . ," Barn started, then paused.

Were they in danger? Yes, they were in danger. He knew the statistics. One was far more likely to die in a car or in a train accident than to die from shark attack. Easier to die of accidental poisoning, or the flu, or a bike crash. But did that mean it was a good idea to surf where sharks had been spotted in the water as recently as the day before? No way. Not after what he had seen out on the boat with Dr. Fitzgibbon.

"It's a bad idea," Barn said after a second. "I mean, they could surf for the next fifty years and never have a problem. Or they could get hit by a shark right now. I guess it's just percentages and risk. If people keep surfing, there will be another attack eventually. That's just the way it is."

"Isn't the water awfully cold for sharks?" Margaret asked.

"It's early in the year. Usually the sharks come up this

way in August, but they can be here now. They start arriving in late May or June. It coincides with the seals giving birth. Great whites are endothermic poikilotherms. That means they create their own heat and regulate their body temperatures. Most fish are cold-blooded, meaning they have the same temperature as the water. Great whites are different. They can range all the way up to Nova Scotia."

"Is there an advantage to being a poiklio . . . What did you call them?" Finn asked.

"Poikilotherm. It means they can devote more energy to hunting than warming up their bodies for other activities. The most gnarly thing about great whites is something called oophagy. The firstborn babies sometimes eat their weaker siblings while the siblings are still eggs. Great whites are born hungry."

"That kid just had a good ride," Margaret said, pointing at one of the surfers. "The bigger one."

"I'm going to call the police," Barn said. "I think it's the right thing to do."

"Will they get in trouble?" Margaret asked.

"I don't think so. I'm not sure. But how would we feel if something happened and we had ignored it?"

He tapped in 911 on his phone. The operator asked if it was an emergency. Hc said no and was redirected to a secondary number. He spoke the number aloud so that Margaret and Finn could help him remember it. Then he tapped in that number. After three rings, an operator came on and asked him to state his business.

"There are some surfers in the water at Wellfleet Beach."

"How many?" the operator asked.

It was a male operator with a flat voice.

"Three," Barn said.

"Are they there now?"

"Yes."

"All right. I'm sending a car. What's your name, please?"

Barn told him.

"Stay right there if you would, sir. An officer will be with you shortly."

Sir?

Barn nearly laughed. *Sir?* But he didn't have time to worry about it, because a police Jeep suddenly appeared on the beach. It must have been nearby, Barn figured, or some sort of magic. Maybe they were on high alert. The Jeep came down the hard-packed sand above the high tide line and stopped. It squawked an electric burp twice, and then the officer inside the vehicle spoke into a microphone.

"Come into shore. Surfers, come into shore. Attention, attention, come into shore."

The surfers didn't pay any attention. Or maybe they didn't hear the officer. One of the surfers actually paddled away from shore. A young female officer stepped out of the vehicle, looked around, and came over to speak with Barn and Finn and Margaret.

"Did you call this in?" the officer asked.

She was short and solid, with her auburn hair pulled back in a ponytail. She had dark eyebrows and alert blue eyes. She wore a lot of equipment on her belt. Her name tag said Officer Van Dusen.

"I called it in," Barn said, standing. "I wasn't sure if I needed to."

"No, it's a good thing you did. They shouldn't be—"

The remaining officer in the vehicle hit the siren. It

blared for a ten count before shutting down. When the siren halted, Officer Van Dusen continued.

"—out there. It's a bad idea."

"Are they in trouble?" Margaret asked, also standing and brushing off the seat of her pants.

"No, no one wants to get them in trouble. They're locals. We know who they are."

The officer in the vehicle hit the siren again. This time the surfers couldn't pretend not to hear it. One after another they paddled toward the beach. The tallest surfer caught a ride and then bailed about fifty feet out. The two other riders rode the waves in on their bellies. When they reached the beach wash, they detached their ankle tethers and picked up their boards.

Barn's instinct was to let the police handle it, but Finn bounced up and trailed Officer Van Dusen toward the water. Margaret looked at Barn, shrugged, then went after Finn. Barn felt the impulse to be nosy, but something about the situation didn't sit right with him. He wasn't sure what it was, but he took a deep breath before following. At the same time, the second officer—the one who had blared the siren from the police Jeep—climbed out and headed toward the surfers, too. The officer was a huge blond man with a crisp crew cut. Maybe he was in his mid-thirties, Barn guessed. His arms looked like he was a body builder. His name tag, when he joined Barn on the way to the surfers, read OFFICER CALHOUN.

"You called it in?" Officer Calhoun asked. "Is that what I heard?"

"Yes, sir."

"Everybody is shark-a-fied," the cop said. "Most beaches you yell 'Shark' and people run out of the water. On Cape Cod, you yell 'Shark' and everyone runs toward the water."

Barn flushed. Did the cop think Barn had joined the bandwagon of people who had gone GWS-nuts on Cape Cod? Or worse, did the cop think going in the water wasn't a bad idea? Barn had to gather himself.

"I thought it was the right thing to do," Barn said simply.

"Hmmmm," Officer Calhoun said.

And then they heard the raised voices of the surfers.

74

"Who called you? You can't close a beach. No one can close the ocean, dude. This is ridiculous."

The leader of the group of surfers was a tall, gangly kid with long, stringy black hair. Probably around seventeen, Barn figured. He had a big nose and a prominent chest bone in the middle of his body, and Barn couldn't help thinking he resembled a T. rex. He had a band of tattoos around his right shoulder and biceps that came to a head—a cobra head on his back—and his bathing suit drooped way down on his body.

"Vince," Officer Van Dusen said, trying to calm him. "Just take it easy."

"I'm not going to take it easy. This is America! We're supposed to be free in this country! If I want to go in the ocean, I can go in the ocean. Liberty and the pursuit of happiness, right? Isn't that in the Constitution?"

"Don't go crazy with your argument, Vince. You saw the signs. The beach is closed."

"Says who? We don't say the beach is closed. Not me and my boys here. We don't say it's closed. We say it's open. We say it's always open. This is so wrong!"

Vince's T. rex face had turned red with passion. He seemed genuinely upset. Officer Van Dusen slowly shook her head.

"It may be wrong and it may be right, but rules are rules. We're only enforcing what the town administration wants us to enforce."

"'Cause one kid gets chomped," one of the surfers behind Vince said, brushing his hair out of his eyes. "Man, that is so unfair."

The kid looked like a miniature copy of Vince, only

heavier. Barn wondered if the kid was Vince's brother. The other kid, a solid guy with a barbed-wire tattoo around his neck that ran down to his arms, didn't speak.

"Look," Officer Calhoun said, stepping into the circle made by the surfers and Officer Van Dusen. "Doesn't matter what we think. Doesn't matter what you think. The beach is closed. You see those signs? Closed."

"There are always going to be sharks, man!" Vince said, pushing strands of hair behind his ears. "This stinks. This is so unfair."

"Did they call you?" the kid with the barbed-wire tattoo asked, pointing at Barn and Margaret and Finn. "These dweebs?"

"Doesn't matter who called us," Officer Van Dusen said in an official voice. "We're here now. That's what counts. We're going to impound your boards. We'll keep them safe until you need them again."

"What are you talking about? You can't do that."

"That's the policy. You can pick them up at the police station when the beach reopens. You have to have a parent sign for them."

Vince threw his board down. He kicked sand on it. Barn tried to signal Margaret and Finn that they should get going, but they were too invested in what was happening to pay attention to him.

"Clean the board off, Vince," Officer Van Dusen said, a little anger slipping into her voice and expression. "We're not the bad guys here. We're just enforcing the closure."

Vince shook his head. The other two dropped their boards and kicked sand over them. It was petty and stupid, but if they had to lose their boards temporarily, then they were going to make it a pain for the officers to bring them to the station.

"Let's get going," Barn whispered to Finn and Margaret.

"Let's get going," Vince said in a mocking voice. "Come on, we have to turn some more people in to the police! You're a tattletale, man. No one likes a tattletale."

"Sorry," Barn said. "I didn't mean—"

"You'll get yours," the miniature version of Vince cut him off. "You don't get to come on to our beach and tell us what to do."

"That's right," the solid guy agreed. "Payback is going to hurt."

Officer Calhoun stepped between the surfers and Barn's group.

"Knock it off," he said. "Do you think it's wise to threaten them in front of us? Someone would have called it in eventually. Obey the rules and we don't have this problem. How many times have we been down a road like this one, Vince?"

"Maybe we would have been finished by the time someone else called," Vince said. "These jerks are little do-gooders."

"And maybe a shark would have already bitten your behind," Officer Van Dusen said. "They did you a favor. You never know."

"And we'll do a favor back for them," mini Vince said. "Easy-peasy."

Barn walked away. He never liked the sound of people arguing. It stressed him out. He was cold and tired and upset. He hadn't meant to cause a conflict, but that was the clear result of calling the police. He could still hear Vince as he walked in the other direction. Barn wondered if he should tell his mother what happened. She would want to know, but he didn't want to spoil her vacation. He put it on a mental shelf. He would decide later.

Margaret ran up and fell into step beside him. Finn came a moment later.

"I hate fighting," Barn said, his face tight with emotion.

"You didn't do it to get them in trouble," Margaret said. "You did it to protect them."

"They don't see it that way," Barn said. "They think I'm a tattletale."

"You're not. Tell him, Finn. It's not the same thing, is it?"

"Barn's a tattletale," Finn said, deadpan. "I hate him."

That made Barn laugh despite himself. He stopped and put his face in his hands and rubbed. Margaret laughed. She grabbed Barn's hands and pulled them away from his face. Then she put one of her hands on her forehead like a shark fin and did a few dance steps.

"Oh yes, we're shark dancing!" Finn said.

"Drop it," Barn said.

"No, come on. Be the shark, Barn," Margaret said. "Tuck into your inner shark!"

Reluctantly, Barn put his hand to his forehead.

It was ridiculous. But because it was ridiculous, it was also kind of funny. Finn and Margaret danced around him, pretending to bite, pretending to swim at him. To defend himself, he put his hand more firmly against his forehead and began the shark dance.

Absurd.

But fun. He danced around in a circle, and Margaret and Finn danced, too. It was only after they had danced for a second that Barn realized maybe Vince and his buddies were right. He was a dweeb. So were Finn and Margaret. Dweebs doing a shark dance on a rainy afternoon at Wellfleet Beach.

The great white patrolled the drop-off.

The drop-off was an underwater cliff, a place where the land gave way to the sandier bottom of the open sea. It ran like a crooked seam thirty yards away from two mounds of black rocks that the seals used for sunning and birthing. The shelf of rock went abruptly from a depth of ten feet to almost fifty. It made a perfect ambushing habitat for the whites to hunt in. They lurked below, and when the seals crossed from shallow water to the deeper zone, the whites exploded upward.

Sometimes the seals resembled surfboards.

Or surfboards resembled seals.

The female white swam calmly, now and then rolling slightly to gaze upward at the surface. Seals could swim as fast—and more nimbly than the white—so the white counted on ambush. If the seals spotted the shark, they would likely swim close to it and dart in and out, pointing it out to other members of their group. Occasionally seals or sea lions ganged together to chase off a white once they spotted it. Today, however, the shark had managed to get into position without being noticed by the seals.

It was an old contest.

Two types of seals inhabited the water off Wellfleet. Gray seals, capable of reaching a length of eight feet and a weight of nine hundred pounds, dominated the area. Gray seals ranged from the Baltic, Western Europe, to Canada and the Northeastern United States. In recent years, gray seal numbers had increased along the Eastern Seaboard, although it was unclear to researchers whether the increase was the result of Canadian populations simply moving south. Called horseheads by sailors, gray seals have long, pointed snouts.

Harbor seals, lighter and shorter than gray seals, with more compact heads, birthed their young in late May and early June. Harbor seal pups could swim within minutes of their birth, and they often accompanied their mothers on hunting expeditions. Sometimes they simply treaded water while the mother dove after cod or mack-erel or eels or lobster.

The white knew none of this, of course.

The white hunted, its annual migration tied to the birthing colo-nies of harbor seals in late May or early June. Pups, in their inexpe-rience, often made hunting easy. Knocked into the water, or separated from their mothers, the white could fly up at the unsus-pecting pup and consume it in a bite.

At sunset, or at dawn, the hunting equation tipped in the shark's favor. The dull light made it easier to cruise below the seals and escape detection. On this day, however, the overcast sky opened the hunting window wider.

It was at 10:37 a.m. that the shark shot up from the bottom of the sea at the small, delicate outline of a baby harbor seal. Water surged past its rough skin, and its tail thrashed the water from side to side. Five feet from collision with the seal, its eyes rolled back in its head. It opened its mouth. The mouth contained fifty full teeth in its gums, twenty-six in its top jaw and twenty-four in its lower jaw. At that exact instant, the shark was effectively blind, which gave the seal its only chance of escape. Dodging quickly, the seal left the water, hopping into the air with incredible skill for a young creature, and landed seven feet northwest of the gaping shark mouth.

The white snapped its jaws shut, anticipating the satisfying crunch of a body, but instead came away with nothing. It did not leave the water after the seal, but swirled down and away. Three nearby seals scattered, and a large gray seal made a chirping sound of alarm. The white's dorsal fin, sixteen inches tall, cut the surface like a knife through a plastic bag filled with water.

A moment later, the white submerged and looped toward the beach. The seals swam after the white, tracking it and making sure it left the area.

10

Barn woke, unsure of where he was or what was happening.

Something loud and thick pounded on the walls of Gail's house, but in the darkness, in the unfamiliar guest room, Barn could not place it.

"Barn?" he heard his mother call.

Her voice sounded scared and uneasy.

He used his phone as a flashlight to guide him to a bedside lamp. He flicked it on. The pounding sound came again. If it had been winter, Barn might have thought it was hail or snow or sleet falling off the roof.

It sounded like something climbing the walls of the house, or knocking to get in, and Barn felt scared and disoriented.

"They're egging us!" Barn heard Gail shout, her voice a mixture of wonder and annoyance. "That's what it is."

She had a bedroom on the ground floor.

Barn pulled a blanket off the bed and wrapped it around him. He hurried downstairs. Gail stood in the kitchen, her phone already against her ear. She wore a light blue robe and her hair was in disorder. Barn's mom came into the kitchen behind him. She wore a robe, too, a red one with white piping.

The pounding stopped.

"Those little cretins!" Gail said, now furious.

"Are you sure it's eggs?" Barn's mom asked, obviously still partially asleep. "What in the world?"

Barn peeked out the window. It was too dark to see anything clearly, but he had a good idea of who might be behind it. A car honked its horn in a long, merry blat. Barn heard kids yelling and laughing. They honked until their sound disappeared in the night.

"They're gone," Barn said, turning back to face the two women.

"Yes, police, yes," Gail said into the phone. She held up her finger to Barn, indicating he should wait a moment before going on.

She gave the police her address. She told them to hurry.

"Eggs!" Gail said as she clicked off. "We've been egged!"

"Egged? I couldn't tell . . . ," Barn's mom said.

"How stupid. I have a security camera. They'll be right in focus in the frame. Ridiculous. I haven't seen anyone egg anything in years."

"It's usually around Halloween, isn't it?" Barn's mom asked.

"I'm pretty sure I know who did it," Barn said. "I think it was done by some kids I met on the beach today."

Both women stopped and turned to him.

"What's that about, Barn?" his mom asked him.

Before he could answer, the police arrived. They made amazing time. They had also arrived on the beach quickly the day before. Barn glanced at his phone. It was 3:33 in the morning. Either too early or too late. Gail went around the house turning on lights. She flicked on the outside lights for the police.

"I'm going to make coffee," Barn's mom said. "Do you want to tell me what's going on, Barn?"

"Some kids at the beach today," Barn said, half his attention focused on the sound of the police talking on the front step. Gail's voice came through. A moment later, Gail returned to the kitchen with a young officer behind her. The officer wore a gray shirt with blue trousers. He looked to be in his mid-twenties. He was short and squat, with a crew cut and thick, muscular arms. He had a small scar over his right eyebrow. His name badge said OFFICER BANKS.

"Morning," he said.

Although it was technically morning, it felt more like night to Barn.

"Officer Banks . . . this is Officer Banks, everyone. This is Jane Whimbril and her son, Barn. Oh, thank goodness you're making coffee, Jane. Smart girl. I was telling Officer Banks that Barn seemed to know who might be behind this egging. Is that true, Barn?"

"I think so."

Officer Banks pulled out a pad of notepaper and unclipped a pen from his breast pocket.

"You want to tell me?"

Barn related the story about the beach as accurately as he could. Officer Banks began nodding when he heard the names of the locals involved.

"Vince Kamur," he said, nodding harder. "He's well known to us. So is his posse."

"I probably have it on camera," Gail said. "I have an elaborate security system in place, and it's never been of any use to me except in this moment."

"Who wants coffee? Cream, sugar?" Barn's mom asked.

It took a few minutes to pass out coffee. Barn grabbed an orange juice from the fridge. Now that the worry about what was happening had passed, Barn thought it felt exciting to be awake so early. The rest of the world was sleeping, and he was awake in the small light of the kitchen, looking out and waiting.

"Power wash is the way to go," Officer Banks said, accepting a cup and tucking his notepad away. "With strong pressure, it should come right off."

"Do these kids get into a lot of mischief?" Barn's mom asked, stirring a coffee with cream for Gail.

"More than their share. Family situations are not ideal," Officer Banks said, then turned to Gail. "We know where to find that crew."

"It's so stupid, though," Gail said, accepting a cup of coffee from Barn's mom. "They must know they'd be caught."

"They want attention," Officer Banks said. "They don't know that they want it, but that's what they want. They're not bad kids, exactly. Just bored and they fail to think things through."

Barn sat at the large kitchen table while Officer Banks exchanged cards and information with Gail. Barn wanted to say that maybe Vince and his boys craved attention, but they also wanted revenge. It made him uncomfortable to think about it. Barn's mom came to sit beside him. A moment later, Gail came back from walking out the officer and slid into her seat at the head of the table.

"I'm sorry, Gail," Barn said. "I had no idea this would spiral out of control like this."

"You didn't do anything. Besides, this is the most excitement we've had around here in years! I even get to use my security system for once. It cost a bloody fortune to install, and everyone assured me I absolutely needed it. That was five years ago! I'll be as curious as anyone to see if it works."

"We'll cover the cost of the power washing," Barn's mom said.

"You'll do nothing of the sort. My homeowner's insurance will pay for it. My insurance agent happens to be a fan of my novels."

"I know this sounds completely nuts," Jane said, "but I am absolutely famished! Would anyone else eat some pancakes if I cooked some up? I'm a little famous for my pancakes. And I think we have some blueberries."

"Yes, please!" Gail said. "Yes, pancakes and bacon. Barn, you've made an enemy! A rich life demands we make a few enemies along the way. If you don't have a few enemies, you're not trying hard enough."

Gail reached across and put her hand on top of Barn's. Barn felt relief. The last thing he wanted was to cause Gail any trouble. He was relieved she was being such a good sport about everything. At the same time, he wondered if the whole episode wasn't going to make Vince even more intent on revenge. It was like an old movie Barn had once watched with his aunt Jupiter. A hero with a sword chopped a bad guy in half, but then the two halves of the bad guy rose up to fight. And then two more each time another guy was chopped in half, and more and more. Vince wasn't going to go away easily.

"I'll cook the bacon," Barn volunteered to get his mind off the situation.

"Pancakes and bacon and heaps of butter and syrup!" Gail said. "Oh, this is living! By the way, the officer told me there's going to be a memorial service for the boy who was killed by the shark. People have started putting wreaths and flowers on the beach."

"Sometimes you forget the tragedy at the center of this," Barn's mom said. "Because there is so much talk about the shark, you forget that a boy died."

Barn nodded. He had a piece of bacon in his hand, ready to put it on the frying pan. He nodded again. His mom was right. He was guilty of that. Guilty of over-looking the boy's death and concentrating on the shark. It was a good reminder.

"I'd like to put some flowers on the memorial site," Barn said. "I'll do that this morning."

Barn was on the phone with his friends. They weren't around that day because it was time to tour the colleges. So they Skyped. He stood next to the beach memorial for Jimmy Xanthopoulous. He had collected wildflowers, and his mom had helped him arrange them into a bouquet. It wasn't much, but Barn felt glad that he had honored Jimmy's memory. People had placed teddy bears and ribbons in a mound near where the attack had occurred. A number of handwritten notes stuck up from the pile of flowers and wreaths.

We love you, Jimmy.

We miss you, Jimmy.

Barn read every note.

Then Finn had called, and Barn had walked away a respectable distance to take the call. Barn told him about the egg attack. Finn was all over it. He wanted to retaliate, and he spent some time going through a list of ways to get back at Vince. Barn listened but didn't join in the discussion. For one thing, he had no appetite to fight back against Vince. And for another, he felt shaky from visiting Jimmy Xanthopoulous's memorial. Jimmy was a boy and he was dead and a shark had done it. It mixed Barn up to think about it all.

When Finn finally ran out of revenge plots, Margaret Valley popped onto the screen. She had on a Boston College baseball hat. She smiled. Seeing her brightened Barn's morning. He smiled back at her.

"Did Finn tell you how boring this is?" she whispered. "Visiting colleges is boring as anything!"

"When will you be back?"

"Tonight. I guess the traffic going over the Sagamore Bridge onto the Cape can be intense, so we have to time it right. I love colleges, but touring more than one at a time is torture."

"Sorry."

"It's not your fault, Barn. What's going on there?"

"Heading out to do some tagging with Jessup. I wish he had been there with us when we ran into Vince and those guys. They wouldn't have talked to him like that."

"Are they going to reopen the beach?"

"It looks like it. I guess the business pressure around here forced the town administrators to reopen the beach. And it's going to be sunny, so the place should be jammed. People are nervous. They have signs up and down the beach that say swim at your own risk. It's weird. I talked to a guy on the beach who walks every morning with his golden retriever, and he doesn't throw a tennis ball far out in the waves anymore. He's worried about his dog."

"That's scary," Margaret said.

"And they did this beach memorial for Jimmy Xanthopoulous. The boy killed in the attack. I just visited it."

"It's terrible to think about. Are you okay, Barn? You sound a little sad."

Was he okay? He wasn't sure. The flowers scattered on the beach had struck something deep inside him. The gulls calling made it all seem intensely sad and lonely. He couldn't put his finger on it, but he was touched that Margaret asked about his feelings.

"I'm okay. Just figuring things out," he said.

"Well, we'll be back tonight. We'll see you then, okay? Don't be sad. I don't want you to be sad."

Then she had to go. She pointed the phone at Finn once more, let him wave, then turned it back to herself. She waved, too.

He walked back to the house. As he arrived, his mom stepped onto the porch with the Scrabble board under her arm. She put the game down on the table by the gas heater.

"Another match?" Barn asked. "You guys are wild and crazy."

"We both like Scrabble."

She shrugged and smiled. Sunlight had already started to heat up the porch.

"How was the beach?" she asked. "Did you put your flowers on the memorial?"

"I did. It's sad."

"Of course it is. You have a big heart, Barn."

She stepped over and hugged him. Usually he got a little itchy when his mom hugged him, but not this morning. He put his head on her shoulder. They stood together for a minute. She was his mom. She kissed his forehead when she let him go. She smiled at him.

"What time is Jessup picking you up?" she asked.

"Around noon."

"And you're going out with this fellow Pokey to tag sharks?"

Barn nodded. The plan was awesome. He couldn't wait to go.

"You're a lucky boy," she said, then sat at the table. She motioned for him to take a seat, too. He did. She smiled at him. It was the kind of smile she used when she wanted to talk about something. She sat forward on the chair, her back straight.

"Can I talk to you about something before the day gets away from us?"

"I won't go in the water. Maybe to get my knees wet, but not much more. I promise."

She smiled. Then she looked down for a moment at her hands.

"It's actually about something else, but it concerns you."

"Okay."

She took a deep breath.

"Jessup asked me out."

Barn stared at her. He wasn't sure he understood. Actually, that wasn't quite true. He understood, but he did not understand. *Jessup had asked her out?* One by one the words made sense, but they seemed to remain like Scrabble tiles, disorganized and refusing to form into a coherent sentence. He felt like a cartoon dog who had to shake his head to unscramble his thoughts.

"Out?" was all he could manage to say.

She nodded.

"I don't know," she said. "I admit when you stand us side by side we might not be two people you would put together. At least not on the face of it. I'm a high school English teacher, and he's a fish-and-game sort of guy."

"He's a biologist."

"Yes, a biologist. And he wears a machete on his leg half the time."

"That's for his job."

She took a deep breath again. She slowly reached over and took his hand.

"He wants to go out on a date, Barn. You know. A date date. I told him I wanted to clear it with you first before I agreed to go with him. I don't mean that you get to say yes or no on my behalf, but I want to take your feelings into consideration."

"I like Jessup fine," he said. "He's a great guy."

That was all he could think to say.

"I know you like him. And he's your friend and supervisor and he thinks the world of you. But we seem to hit it off. We laugh a lot. I'd like to accept his offer, but I don't want it to be awkward for any of us."

Finally it all clicked in. He felt as if he had just snapped out of a dream. His mom wanted to go out on a date with Jessup Sabine. He squeezed his mom's hand. He had sort of seen this coming, but it had been murky.

He loved his mom more than anything in the world. Whatever made her happy made him happy.

"I think it's great, Mom. You should go out with him. Outside of work, you two have a lot in common."

She collapsed against the back of the chair.

Barn smiled. "So, you're going out on a date with a guy who wears a machete? Is that what I'm hearing?"

Mom laughed. "I guess that's what I'm saying," she said, blushing.

He put his hand across the table and took her hand and squeezed.

"It's great, Mom. I mean it. I'm happy for you both."

"Well, it's not as if we're getting married, Barn. We're just going to dinner."

She didn't say anything else. Barn sat near her, watching the sun move across the water, the gulls calling and searching for food just beyond the breakers. It had been quite a morning, he thought. Quite a night, too. In a while, he was going to go out with Jessup and tag sharks. He hoped things didn't become awkward between Jessup and him. He didn't think they would. It was a lot to think about.

A few minutes later, Gail came onto the porch.

"I'm determined to beat you, Janey!" she said, smacking her palm lightly against the Scrabble board. "Be warned!"

Barn watched them play for a while, letting the sun climb onto his skin, watching the people slowly converge on the beach like ants coming to a picnic.

Pokey Bob Crescent could have been a pirate.

He was tall and skinny with a beard that reached almost to his belt. He wore three beaded bands around his beard. He went barefoot on board his boat, the *Gray Jay*, and his skin had been weathered into a rough, leathery brown that reminded Barn of an old library couch. A pair of snap-apart, snap-together reading glasses interrupted the pirate vibe, but otherwise he could have been a pirate from two centuries before. He had a wicked-thick Maine accent. Barn liked him immediately.

Between Jessup's Southern drawl and Pokey Bob's

Maine twang, Barn had trouble understanding a word. Luckily, Dr. Fitzgibbon was on the boat with them. On the ride out to the tagging zone, Dr. Fitzgibbon explained how the tagging runs worked.

"We usually start along Monomoy, which is a spit of sandy land that comes off the crook of Cape Cod's elbow. Sports fishermen call it Shark Alley, but we don't like to promote that name. There is a delicate balance between making the public aware of the sharks and turning their presence into a carnival."

"And the seals are right there," Barn said, spotting the first brown bodies basking in the sunlight.

"Right there. We're trying to take a census of the white shark population, but it's an estimate at best. We're doing an acoustic check today. We put out sensors and then any tagged shark that passes by pings the sensor. Bluetooth, just like in your car or on your phone. We can determine which shark it is and we can figure out who is in the water, who is passing by, and so on. Scratchy and Mr. Frisky, for instance, have been recorded around here for the past three years. They return every summer. If we examine those data, and extrapolate, we can make a solid guess about shark numbers."

"And it's all about the return of the seals?"

"Mostly. They were on the edge of extinction in this area, but legislative protections brought them back. It's a rich marine environment. We get minke whales and bird life, very rich bird life, and because of that there is some confusion. The public sees a fin, and immediately they assume it's a great white. We have to err on the side of caution. Our current best guess is a population of about two hundred white sharks off the Cape Cod coast. That could be wrong by a fair number on either side of the guess. But it gives us a working benchmark."

"With those numbers, it means attacks on humans are going to continue to occur."

"Probably yes. I'm afraid so. You never know, of course, but the two worlds overlap. Some of the fishermen have been hooking into sharks along here. The other day a pair of insurance underwriters out of Boston had a white come up and inspect their boat. Rattled them."

The *Gray Jay* cut back its engines, and the wake and choppy sea kicked the boat back and forth. A small spotter plane slowly buzzed into view. The plane flew low over the water, scanning for whites. When it spotted one, it called down the shark's location to the *Gray Jay*. Then, if the shark had no tag, Pokey Bob ran out on the pulpit, the long extension from the bow of the boat, and did his best to insert an acoustic device into the dorsal fin. That was the game plan.

For Barn, it was heaven.

It didn't take long. Ten minutes after cutting back the engines, the plane radioed down that they had spotted a shark 150 yards to the northwest.

"You coming out with me?" Pokey Bob asked.

He spoke from the central cabin above Barn. Barn had to shade his eyes to see him.

"Coming out where?" Barn asked.

"Out on the pulpit. Let's go."

Barn felt his brain go a bit wavy. It was the second time today that someone had spoken to him, and he had understood their words, but he failed to click everything together.

First his mother had said she was going out on a date with Jessup. Now this.

Barn nodded. He wasn't exactly sure what his nod meant.

He needn't have worried. Jessup reached up to Pokey Bob and grabbed a harness and began fitting it over Barn's head. Barn found himself holding up his hands like a little kid whose mom was yanking down his sweater. Only this was no sweater. It was a harness to attach him to the boat.

"And here's your clip," Jessup said, handing Barn one end of a cord that obviously attached to something on the pulpit. "You don't take it off until you're back safely on the main floor of the boat. Understand?"

"Yes."

"Safety first. Pokey Bob will take good care of you."

Jessup slapped him on the shoulder. Apparently, Barn was properly equipped to do whatever he was supposed to do. He gathered that whatever it was had to take place on the long, skinny walkway that extended off the bow of the *Gray Jay*. He carried the connecting strap in his right hand

and hurried forward. Pokey Bob stood at the entrance to the pulpit. He smiled.

"Ready to walk the plank, Barn?" asked Pokey Bob.

"Absolutely."

"Clip on here after I head out. We'll see what we can do."

Barn finally understood. The long metal pulpit provided a darting platform that extended straight out from the front of the *Gray Jay*. The platform was narrow and made of metal, like a radio or cell tower set on its side. The railing on the right was nothing more than a metal cable to which you attached your safety carabiner. Barn did as he was told after Pokey Bob stepped onto the pulpit and explained what was going to happen.

"I'll get all the way out. You can come up pretty near me, but not too near. I need room to maneuver, and I don't want to have to worry about where you are. See what I mean? You'll be able to see everything. If you see something I've missed, shout out. I don't think this shark has been tagged. It's not giving off a signal. Course, it could be a mermaid. You never know."

Pokey Bob winked and cuffed Barn on the shoulder.

Barn nodded and checked the carabiner again. It was securely fastened.

Then Pokey Bob scrambled out along the pulpit. He was long and lean, but he seemed to come to life once he was headed out on a tagging mission. Barn followed. His heart beat hard in his chest. The pulpit was narrow. His hips barely cleared the side cables. He paused a moment out of fear once he had stepped two strides away from the boat. He looked down . . .

. . . and saw . . .

. . . nothing but water.

He took a deep breath. He knew he had to decide to be brave or give in to the fear of walking a thin metal walkway over dark ocean water. It was one thing to talk about sharks and look at their behavior on the Global Shark Attack File, but it was another to stand on a tiny platform fifteen feet above the ocean with a half pirate like Pokey Bob. He could always imagine the bull sharks down in Florida, the glide of a big one as it went beneath him and lifted him slightly into the air.

He took another deep breath. Then a third. In that

moment, he felt his nervousness, his fear, give way to the pure exhilaration of standing above the rolling Atlantic, sharks potentially nearby, the wind like a slap across his face every time he turned his cheek to look around. If it wouldn't have been so corny, he would've raised his fists and danced around. Maybe do his famous shark dance with his hand held to his forehead like a fin, but then he simply felt himself becoming wild and empty and happy.

"Over there!" Pokey Bob shouted.

He pointed to his left. The boat turned gently in that direction.

In that instant, Barn saw the great white.

Tears came into his eyes. He didn't know what that was all about, and he tried to blame it on the wind, but he also knew something about sharks helped him when he felt lonely or down about something in his life. Sharks inspired him. They taught him. They demonstrated to him the beautiful intricacy of nature.

He studied and absorbed all the details he could about the shark as he inched forward to watch Pokey Bob take a try at tagging it. He had never felt more alive.

13

It was a juvenile, maybe seven feet long.

Probably male.

It swam just below the surface, the waves occasionally lifting it and making it more visible. Barn fought down the impulse to pull out his phone and take a picture. He didn't want to be a tourist. He wanted to *see* the shark, his first GWS, in all its sleek beauty.

"It's a little spooked by the boat," Pokey called, making a motion with his free hand to throttle down. "Ease up the engine. Maybe it will come by."

The shark swam in a lazy circle away from the boat.

From Pokey's platform, the shark remained perhaps twenty yards away. Barn calculated that the tagging spear was about ten feet long. That meant they had to close on the shark quietly, trying to keep it interested, letting the shark's inbred curiosity put it in position for tagging. It was a tricky balance. The shark could spook and be gone in a millisecond.

"Easy, easy, easy," Pokey said, his voice barely loud enough to hear over the slosh of water against the *Gray Jay*.

Barn leaned out to see the shark better.

It was the most beautiful thing he had ever seen.

It fit the standard pattern for whites: gray-green on top, white below. Positioned as it was, facing away from the boat, Barn couldn't see the shark's classic grin, but the size and thickness of the first dorsal fin astonished him. It was big. Barn knew it connected to the frame of the shark by cartilaginous rods, called ceratotrichia, which helped support the strength and rigidity of the fin. Without the pair of dorsal fins—the second one, called a caudal fin, located between the first dorsal

fin and the tail—the shark would not have the keel—
the heavy V-shaped bottom of a sailboat—required to
keep it properly positioned in the water. It also wouldn't
be able to turn and hunt with the agility he knew the
shark possessed. The design of the body was a perfect
thing.

But it was something else that made Barn take special
notice.

The shark saw him.

It did. It was conscious of him. Barn would have sworn
to it. For an instant, as he leaned out to examine the shark,
as the boat edged closer and as Pokey Bob lifted his tagging spear, Barn knew the shark grew aware of them. He
already knew sharks were not ravenous beasts who ate
everything in the water or came flying out of the sky in
tornadoes. That was ridiculous.

But what he hadn't been prepared for was the intense
awareness the shark sent back to him. He knew fishermen
gave accounts of white sharks rolling slightly to look at
the people on board. Whites did it to see seals on land or
birds sitting on the surface. Barn knew the white had

rolled slightly to see them. They were not sneaking up on the shark after all.

The shark let them approach. It was confident in its own superiority.

Suddenly, Pokey Bob's spear flashed forward, and the old pirate let out a loud whoop. The plane above wagged its wings. The shark, darted with an acoustic tag, shot off into deeper water, startled more than hurt.

"Bingo!" Pokey Bob shouted. "Perfect tag. Right at the base of the dorsal."

"We've got his signal," Dr. Fitzgibbon called. "We're already tracking him. He went deep."

"How did you like that, Barn?" Pokey Bob asked, coming back toward him. He carried the tagging spear in his left hand. The scrape of his carabiner made a metal grinding sound as he walked.

"Amazing. Thank you for letting me come out here . . ."

"Makes you think, huh? All this water. Imagine the early sailors? Imagine what it all must have felt like for them. Oh, the briny, briny deep!"

Barn nodded. He half expected Pokey Bob to start

dancing a pirate dance. Obviously he still felt the excitement of the hunt.

"A GWS breeched at a guy out on one of these the other day. Down in Mexico. Like a trout coming up after a mayfly. Left the water entirely and almost rammed into the pulpit. We didn't want to tell you ahead of time."

"Thanks for that, Pokey."

Pokey smiled. He had a warm, happy smile.

"In earlier days, you wouldn't last long if you fell in the water. Too many sharks. Nowadays, the population is so depleted you could probably swim for a day and not worry too much. Well, not a day."

"That shark was . . . ," Barn started, but words failed him.

"Powerful? Majestic? And remember, that's a juvenile. Deep Blue, the biggest white shark ever sighted, is twenty feet long and eight feet tall. Eight feet. Do you understand what that means? Its bottom to its top. You could walk into its mouth without bending over. In fact, you would have to jump to touch the roof of its mouth."

Pokey Bob patted his shoulder. He had a heavy hand.

"Now, we better get you out of the sun, partner. You are cooked."

"I'm always cooked in the sun."

Barn walked back along the pulpit and detached his carabiner. Pokey came on board behind him. Jessup waited, ready to help Barn remove his harness.

"How did you like that?" Jessup asked.

"Awesome. Really awesome."

"It's down about seventy feet and traveling back toward Nauset Beach. How did the tag go, Pokey?"

"Good tag," Pokey said, starting to pull his harness off. "Right at the base of the dorsal."

"He's the Robin Hood of shark taggers," Jessup said. "Here, let me help you get out of that harness."

Barn held his arms up again, and Jessup shucked the harness off him. Little by little, the realization that he had participated in a GWS tagging built up in him. He wanted to text everyone, send pictures, but another part of him, a deeper part of him, remembered how aware the shark had been. That's what he wanted to remember. A photo couldn't represent that. Nothing could recapture that.

Some things were better without a phone stuck to your hand.

Before Pokey had his harness off, Dr. Fitzgibbon stepped out of the captain's cabin and called down to them.

"There's a shark right off the Wellfleet Beach. Ten, twenty feet out. We just got the call."

She pointed to the plane. It had suddenly veered off toward land. Its first duty was to spot sharks that posed a threat to swimmers.

"Let's go," Jessup said.

"We think it's Sweetie Pie," Dr. Fitzgibbon said in an excited voice. "We think she's come back at last."

Barn heard the *Gray Jay*'s engines rev up. *Sweetie Pie*. Even Barn knew the name. She was a legend among shark researchers. Barn steadied himself with one hand on the railing as the boat began to surge through the waves toward land.

14

Even from an eighth of a mile out, Barn saw the commotion right away. The crowd on Wellfleet Beach clustered in a mass a dozen feet away from the water's edge. Obviously, people saw something extraordinary, because they raised their hands and pointed, aimed cameras at the waves, pulled each other by the shoulder to draw their neighbor's attention to something. Crowd behavior.

Barn didn't doubt the reason was Sweetie Pie.

A Wellfleet police Jeep parked close to the water, its blue light turning. The light made a bright blue scratch on the water every time it circled.

"It's her ID number," Dr. Fitzgibbon said, staring at the computer monitor. "If it's not Sweetie Pie, it's another shark wearing her number."

"Or a shark that ate Sweetie Pie, tag and all," Jessup said.

He raised his eyebrows and smiled.

"I'd like to see the shark that could handle her," Pokey Bob said from his place behind the wheel. "That would be a shark for the ages."

Pokey Bob throttled the engine down as they approached the beach. It was easy to figure out where to look, because the people migrated slowly down the sand as the shark progressed along the water's edge. The *Gray Jay* began to roll more forcefully now that it sat just beyond the breakers. Barn felt a tiny stir in his belly. He had never been seasick, but the bobbing of the boat didn't feel great in his gut.

"I can't see her," Dr. Fitzgibbon said, "but her acoustic message is coming in clear as a bell."

"Something is moving through the water," Pokey Bob said, one hand remaining on the wheel, his beard being pushed to one side by the land breeze. "It's dark and big. Could be a seal, but unlikely."

"I can see it," Barn said. "I can see the shark form. See? Wait for when the wave goes up."

It wasn't easy to see, but Barn knew he was correct. Two waves passed before a third one lifted the shark enough above the plane of the ocean. Barn saw the outline of the shark. It was a big animal seemingly in no hurry to be anywhere but where she was.

"It could be Sweetie Pie," Dr. Fitzgibbon said, speaking toward the screen. "Where have you been, my little girl? I can't believe it could be her after all this time."

"Why do they call her Sweetie Pie?" Jessup asked.

"They captured her once," Barn said, still straining to see the shark in the waves. "You know, in one of those capture slings. They brought her next to the boat and tagged her, took her measurements, the usual. But one of the interns happened to rub her belly. She didn't mean to, but when she did, Sweetie Pie's tail moved. Just like scratching a dog's belly and having its paw go up and down. They did it a dozen times and each time her tail flexed. After they released her, she kept coming by the boat. Everyone had the impression she wanted her belly rubbed again. So she got the name Sweetie Pie."

"You know your shark lore, Barn," Jessup said.

"It's actually a simple scratch response. In dogs, anyway. Well, you all probably know it, but it's just the dog reacting to what could be a fly or a tick. No one could say if a shark has a scratch response. As a marine animal, it probably doesn't, but Sweetie Pie's reaction made people wonder."

"We do know they like to scratch, though," Dr. Fitzgibbon said, her attention still on the computer screen. "They like to rub against things. Okay, now she's moving."

Then Barn heard a gunshot.

It came from the beach and sounded like little more than a *pop*. But then six or seven more shots came in rapid fire. It was impossible to know the caliber or strength of the gunfire over the boom of the waves. Barn squinted at each round and saw people run away from the shooter. Then he watched as officers from the Jeep ran toward a man who lowered his rifle. The man had been shooting at

Sweetie Pie. Besides being absurd—the chance of him penetrating through the water and hitting the shark was astronomically low—it bothered Barn to see someone assume he had the right to shoot at an animal that had done nothing to him. And to fire a gun in a public place was completely reckless.

"Stupid, stupid, stupid," Pokey Bob said to the port side. "He's going to hurt someone like that. Might as well fire at the moon."

"He wasn't far off from hitting us," Jessup agreed.

"Now she's moving faster," Dr. Fitzgibbon narrated. "Sweetie Pie. Get going, girl. Don't stick around here with these idiots."

The crowd on the beach had circled back once the police had the shooter in custody. Two more police Jeeps had arrived. The man with the rifle had his hands locked behind his head. Two police officers stood in front of him, apparently arresting him for firing a rifle in a public space. Barn wondered what it was that made some people's first reaction at seeing a shark the desire to kill it. It made no sense to him.

"She's traveling out toward the seals," Dr. Fitzgibbon said, pointing. "Probably wants a bite to eat. She's a big, bonny lass."

"How big is Sweetie Pie?" Jessup asked Barn.

"Last time she was measured she was seventeen feet three inches," Barn said. "That was three years ago, I think. Given an average growth rate, she's probably about eighteen now. Is that about right, Dr. Fitzgibbon?"

Dr. Fitzgibbon nodded.

"That's a big fish," Jessup said.

"Length of a minivan," Barn agreed. "Maybe a little longer."

"She's a big girl, our Sweetie Pie," Dr. Fitzgibbon said. "Such a bonny, bonny lass."

"Let's keep tagging," Pokey Bob said, snapping on the engines. "Let's not get distracted."

Barn suddenly couldn't help himself. He stepped quickly to the side of the boat and threw up. It was a horrible, wonderful feeling. The relief was almost worth the grossness. He took out his handkerchief and wiped his mouth when he finished. The others had stepped away to give him privacy. He tried to even out his breathing, but it was no use. He scrambled to the side of the boat again and threw up. He didn't care. He didn't want to be anywhere else in the world except on that boat, tagging sharks. The shadow of his head made a wavy silhouette on the water's surface.

Sweetie Pie swam with a long, undulating movement that swept her tail three feet on either side of her center line. She was a big shark, with a broad gut and a head as wide as a trash barrel. Three mature pilot fish trailed her head, a haze of fish that lived permanently beside her. The pilot fish lived off the scraps of her kills. They were masters of snatching drifting pellets of flesh from a victim, then hurrying back to Sweetie Pie's shoulder. To prey on a pilot fish, a predator had to get past Sweetie Pie's intimidating mouth. Few predators bothered to try.

Two remora fish — smaller fish, with specially adapted suckers that allowed them to attach to a shark or ray or whale's body — clung to her belly and throat. They ate lice and vermin from the great white's skin and teeth.

Sweetie Pie swam twelve miles per hour. She followed her hunger. She had not eaten in a little over a month. Her last feeding had been on a rotted harbor whale that had died near shore and drifted out to open ocean with the current. She had glutted herself then, ripping enormous bites of the bloated body and swallowing the flesh without chewing. In the space of three days, she fed approximately twenty times. As the days continued, the whale's flesh became less bountiful, and more putrid, but Sweetie Pie's digestive juices easily dissolved the food into a useful stew. Now the stew had been absorbed and she had begun to seek food.

She slowed when she neared the seal's nursery. She dove close to the bottom and swam calmly, trying not to give herself away. The seals appeared above her as bright lines of light when they dove off the rocks. Entering the sea, their bodies bubbled the water and turned it into a bar of refraction. The shark noted the effect.

She swam the length of the ocean fault, keeping to the deep water. As a member of the Lamnidae family of fish, she had evolved the ability to maintain her body temperature a few degrees higher than her environment. Using a system called rete mirabile, which allowed a specific arrangement of blood vessels in the large swimming muscles to transfer heat to the cold blood coming from the gills, she swam comfortably in the forty-seven-degree ocean. Her lateral line—the line on the side of her body that registered fluctuations in water pressure, heat, and movement—sent constant updates to her U-shaped brain.

She had started back in the other direction when the seals finally discovered her. She let them dance around her and swam in her quiet way back toward shore. It was too light for successful hunting. Better to have the light fading. Better to be in the near darkness when the outline of the seals became small clouds on the sky of the open sea, and the shark came deadly toward the air, falling up as dying fish, in their time, always did.

15

"Stand right there. I'll just be a second."

Barn stood on Wellfleet Beach, a reporter and her cameraman conferring quickly about the light and background. They had come to do a news report about the shark attack, the status of the shark population, and the discharge of the rifle earlier in the afternoon. Dr. Fitzgibbon introduced Barn to the reporter. She had referred to him as a shark expert, and he could tell the reporter was disappointed that he was just a kid. But she had a report to file and she had to get something shot. She was a young reporter, maybe mid-twenties, with a bright, happy expression. She wore a navy windbreaker with the station's call letters written in red across the front: WKRB, Boston. Her name was Gloria Abarca.

The cameraman, a tall, goofy-looking young guy named Edgar, had a camera on his shoulder. He had a light meter on a tether around his neck, and he checked it frequently as Gloria moved him around.

"So we're going to shoot you with the water in the background, but don't feel you have to turn and point to anything," Gloria said after she finished discussing the shot with Edgar. "Just be natural. We can cut things as we need them. You know, edit."

"Okay."

"I'll do a little lead-in, then turn to you. Edgar will get it all. If we have to do a second lead-in, we can. You ready?"

"I guess."

Barn looked at his mom, who stood behind the reporters. She met Barn and Jessup when they came in from tagging sharks. Jessup had to run to a meeting. But Barn noticed the way they smiled at each other.

She had to sign a release form to let him be interviewed because he was underage. Now she watched and smiled and sometimes made funny faces at him. Gail stood beside her. A few people had already approached Gail for autographs. Gail handled the people gracefully.

"How do I look?" Gloria asked Edgar.

She put her hands at her sides. Edgar checked her through the camera lens. When he looked back, he told her to fix her hair on the right side. She did. He nodded. They were ready.

"This is Gloria Abarca from Wellfleet Beach in Wellfleet, Massachusetts, and I am standing on the beach where four days ago a young surfer was fatally attacked by a shark while surfing."

She paused for effect and then continued.

"Earlier today, a shark was seen just off the beach here and a man fired several rifle rounds at it. The man has been apprehended and placed in custody. With me is Barn Whimbril, a young man who authorities say knows more about sharks than most biologists. Barn, you were here?"

"I was. I was on a boat just beyond the breakers."

"And from your vantage point, you could see the shark?"

"Just the outline. But the shark had an acoustic tag, so the biologists on board knew its identity."

"With the fatal attack only a few days ago and now the appearance of a second great white shark in the surf here, can you tell us what's going on? Why so many sharks this season?"

Barn nodded. He wasn't sure why he nodded. Kind of unnecessary, but he did it anyway.

"The seal populations have increased, so more sharks are visiting the area. That's really all there is to it. More food, more sharks."

"And do these added sharks add to the increase in likelihood of an attack?"

"Probably. When surfers are on boards, they can resemble seals or even turtles. Most shark attacks on surfers by great white sharks probably occur as accidents. Often a great white will test bite a human and then retreat. They don't like our taste or at least don't recognize it."

"And this was a great white shark?"

"From all indications, yes. The shark yesterday was definitely a GWS."

"A great white shark?"

Barn nodded. Gloria opened her eyes a little wider to get him to speak. He got it.

"Yes, a great white shark."

She stopped. Edgar nodded with his eye still on the screen of the camera. His mother started to clap. He shot her some eye lasers to tell her to stop. She laughed and nodded. Gail grinned.

Gloria straightened her hair again and said, "I'm going to ask you a few more questions that we might want to cut in with the main interview. You okay with that?"

"Sure."

She took her cue from Edgar, who simply nodded that he was ready.

"Authorities are struggling with the question of safety on the local beaches. It's the beginning of summer, and local shops and merchants count on the beach being open to draw tourists. I'm with Barn Whimbril here, who is young, but authorities listen when he speaks. He is a young man who has made sharks the focus of all his studies."

"Not all," Barn said, but then realized he wasn't supposed to speak yet.

"Understanding shark behavior the way you do, Barn, do you think the beach should be closed until the sharks leave the area? What should be done to keep swimmers safe?"

"The sharks will be here all summer. They probably won't start south until September."

Before Barn could say anything else, he sensed something flying toward him. He ducked a little instinctively, and in the next moment, a body smashed into his. The contact came so quickly, and so unexpectedly, that the impact knocked him off his feet and into the air. He landed with a thud in the sand and an orange Frisbee clunked down after him, hitting against his shoulder. His wind had been knocked out of him.

"Oh, oh, sorry, man," someone said near to him. "My bad. Just going after the Frisbee."

It was Vince. Before Barn could move, Vince grabbed

his Frisbee and trotted off. Barn stayed on his back for a second, stunned and finding it difficult to breathe. He didn't think he was hurt.

"Are you okay, honey?" his mom asked, bending over him, her head swiveling to look at wherever Vince had disappeared to, then back at him. "That kid was . . . There should be rules . . . Are you okay?"

Barn nodded. He was too stunned to be able to think clearly.

"Man, he decked you," Edgar said. "You were in the shot, then suddenly you were gone. Pretty cool sequence, actually. I'll send you the clip if you want to see it."

Barn got up. His head hurt and his lungs burned. More than his head, his pride hurt. It was weird to be knocked off your feet by a guy you didn't even really know. Barn dusted himself off. Gloria stepped back so she wouldn't get sand on her. His mom kept her hand on his elbow in case he got dizzy. Gail hadn't moved, but she looked concerned.

In that second, he almost told his mom about Vince. He knew he should tell, but something prevented it. It had something to do with taking responsibility for himself. For fighting his own battles. It confused him to think about it. If he turned to his mother and Gail and said, *Here, you two take care of it*, they would. They would call the police and get the whole cycle going again, get Vince carted off the beach. Barn didn't want that. He couldn't stand that. His dad wouldn't have called out for help, and Barn didn't think he should, either. He had to settle it with Vince. He had to face him down.

"I'm fine, Mom," he said. "Thanks, but I'm okay."

"I think we have everything we need," Gloria said. "Edgar, are you good?"

"I'm good. You want to see that kid hit you? I can play it back."

"No thanks."

"We should report him," his mom said. "Seriously, that was reckless."

It took a few minutes to say goodbye to Gloria and Edgar. They decided to do a few reaction shots with random beachgoers. They said they would text them when they knew when the segment would air, but they expected it to be on both the five and eleven o'clock broadcasts. The station's social media platforms were buzzing with shark news and questions.

Barn walked with his mom and Gail back to the house. His mom linked her arm through his. He didn't mind, because he felt a little shaky. One of his ribs on his right side hurt. His wrist had twisted awkwardly, too, and he flexed his fingers as he walked to get it moving. His breathing eased. Gradually he felt the shock of the contact subsiding.

"You okay?" his mom asked.

"Yes. I'm fine."

"You looked like a quarterback getting blindsided."

"I felt like a quarterback getting blindsided."

They walked a little more. Gail stopped to speak with a neighbor. She told them to go ahead, she would be right along.

When they were alone, his mother turned to him. She smiled. It took her a moment to compose her thought. Barn waited, wondering what was going on. Finally she spoke.

"I'm going out tonight, sweetie."

"With Jessup?"

She nodded.

"Okay," he said. "That's great."

"We're going to dinner. We shouldn't be back late."

"It's fine, Mom. I hope you two have a good time. I'm happy you're going out."

Barn felt himself blush. It was awkward to discuss dating with his mom, but he appreciated her situation. She hadn't dated anyone in a long time. She probably didn't know how to handle it any better than he did.

They kept walking. He was relieved when they approached Gail's house to see two people sitting on the front steps, waiting. Barn started smiling just to see them. The cavalry had arrived just in time.

Finn Moody, his best friend.

And Margaret Valley. The girl who made him smile just by being near.

16

Barn watched Margaret Valley put ketchup on her French fries. He had never seen anyone do it more carefully. She used a squeeze bottle and wove a thin line of ketchup back and forth, making the neatest design Barn had ever seen.

"That's awesome," he said.

Almost everything she did was awesome, honestly. That's what he thought.

"What's awesome?" she asked, her attention still on the paper plate full of fries.

"The way you put ketchup on your fries."

"What's so special about that?"

She didn't look up. He pointed to Finn's fries, then his.

"Look at ours. Ours are a mess."

"I like having a little bit on each fry. If you do it right, it's better."

"You should see her eat spaghetti," Finn said, dabbing his fry in a pool of ketchup on his plate. "Or any kind of pasta. She takes it way, way seriously."

"And corn," she said. "I know I'm weird about corn. I eat around. Not side to side, but around."

"You have issues," Finn said. "Serious squirrel issues."

Barn laughed. Part of the laugh was just from feeling good about having his two friends back beside him. They sat at an outdoor picnic table on Pacho's Quick Take patio. Now and then Barn smelled the deep fry odor of scallops and French fries. Cars passed by, but it had become evening and everything had slowed. It had begun to cool off, too, which was a relief. His skin burned from being in the sun. His skin also burned from thinking about . . .

. . . his mom out on a date with Jessup.

He shut that thought down.

But not all the way. Because his mom and Jessup were out on a date! A date! He was okay with it, he swore to himself, but it still felt weird. Were they going to fall in love and then Jessup would move in and become his stepdad? That was getting way ahead of things, he knew, but thoughts pinged around in his head. Not bad thoughts. Just busy thoughts.

Margaret put the squeeze bottle down. Then she began eating her fries. She ate them one by one with the wooden stabber Pacho's put in all the fry orders. She wore shorts and a pair of flip-flops. Her gray sweatshirt said EMERSON. She had gotten the sweatshirt on one of the college visits.

Finn wore a T-shirt that said NORTHEASTERN. It was pink.

Margaret rearranged her legs under the table. Her leg bumped his.

"Sorry," she said.

"It's okay."

"How are your ribs, man? They still sore?" Finn asked.

"Pretty sore. My wrist hurts more than my ribs."

"That Vince guy is such a jerk," Margaret said. "What's his issue?"

"They're just bored," Finn said. "They don't have much to do around here, I guess. Still, I'd like to tie them to an anthill and cover them with honey and then watch as the ants—"

"I'll get you the honey," Barn interrupted. It felt good to be angry at Vince. "I would so love watching ants crawl all over Vincent Van Gross! Right up his nose."

"Now that's *gross*!" Margaret said.

"Or we could steal his surfboard," Barn said, "and like take pictures of it everywhere around here but don't let him have it back. That would drive him nuts."

"That's no good," Finn said. "Leave the torture to me."

"He deserves something, though," said Barn. "He smashed into me with the Frisbee. That guy has a hard time getting over things. Like, when he's seventy, he's going to be stalking me with a Frisbee."

Barn realized he and Finn had been going a little overboard. He looked at Margaret. She wasn't playing their game.

"There's plenty to do here," Margaret said, picking at her fries. "Are you kidding? Compared to where we live

142

there's much more. They could go into Boston or do anything at all. Instead they hang around here and cause trouble."

"Surfing is their thing," said Barn.

"What time is your interview on TV, Barn?" Margaret asked. "I want to see how you look on camera."

"I'm not sure."

"Yes, you are, you dog," Finn said, and elbowed him. "You know it's on at five. I'll be recording it. Never fear. It's all under control."

"Want to walk back to the beach?" Margaret asked a few minutes later. "We can watch the sunset. And there are a bunch of fishermen out there at this time of night, usually, right?"

Finn nodded. Barn picked up the last of his French fries. He felt a bit shaky still from Vince's attack earlier in the day. And maybe he did feel funny about his mom on a date with Jessup. He wasn't sure about that. It seemed like a lot had happened all at once. All from one phone call. It would have been funny if it wasn't a little scary. Vince and his goons were bigger and stronger and certainly more violent than Barn and his friends. He understood that. Part of him, though, always tried to see things objectively, and he had a hard time rising to the level of anger that motivated Vince. Violent people got away with things, he figured, because other people weren't willing to meet their violence.

It made his stomach churn to think about it.

He tossed the last of his fry boat into the garbage. He watched moths circle the fluorescent light above the snack bar window. The moths resembled caterpillars that had learned to hang glide.

It was a quick walk back to the beach. Margaret was right: A dozen fishermen stood on the beach, their lines out in the surf. The sun had begun to set behind them. Finn had dumped his empty container of fries, too, but Margaret still carried hers and the gulls began to fly near her, begging for a handout. She waved at them as you might wave at flies. It was funny, and Finn called her on it.

"You know you can't just wave away seagulls, right?" he asked.

"They're so greedy. They bug me. What do they want?"

144

"They want fries with just the right amount of ketchup on them."

Margaret grinned. When they reached the beach, Barn found a place to sit on a dune and plopped down. He felt tired and a bit achy. It had been a funny kind of day. It was still a funny kind of day, but he liked having his friends beside him.

"Barn, who takes care of your aquariums when you're away?" Margaret asked, sitting near him.

"They're pretty much okay for a few days, but Lucas will go over if I'm gone longer. I take care of his aquariums if he has to be out of town."

Lucas was his buddy. They shared a passion for raising fish.

For a long minute or two, they sat in silence, watching the waves roll in and out. The fishermen didn't seem to be having much luck. Finn pulled out his phone after a while and texted with his parents. Margaret finished her fries and clapped off her hands to get rid of the salt and grease.

"I'm going to go down to the water and rinse my hands," she said. "BRB."

Be right back.

Barn watched her walk away. He dug his feet in the sand. It felt good. The sand still had some of the day's warmth collected in it. It felt so good that he pushed back and lay down against the slope of the dune. He looked up at the sky. The sun threw light against a few cumulus clouds, but otherwise the evening was perfect.

"That's not good," Finn said, his voice changed to a more serious tone.

"What's not good?" Barn asked, thinking he had come across something on his phone.

"Vince and his boys."

"Where?"

Barn sat up.

A black Jeep Wrangler had suddenly appeared on the beach. It had stopped between the spot where Barn and Finn sat and where Margaret had gone to wash her hands. Barn saw Vince climb out of the driver's seat. The two other guys flanked down to the north and south. If Margaret wanted to get back to them, she had to pass right through them.

"Let's go," Barn said, jumping up.

Finn jumped up beside him.

But it was too late. Margaret made a run down the beach toward where most of the fishermen congregated, but Vince's boys cut her off and turned her back the other way. Barn ran. He heard Margaret shout, but the sound mixed with the gulls. Then he watched Vince bend close to her. She shook her head. A second later, one of Vince's sidekicks pointed at Barn and Finn. Vince smiled. But anytime Margaret tried to step around him, he stepped in front of her and held his hands out like a crossing guard explaining she had to wait for traffic to clear.

Barn ran as hard as he could at Vince. Vince sidestepped in time and stuck his leg out, and Barn piled right into the mounded beach. His face went into the sand, and his body crashed like an accordion behind him. He felt wild with embarrassment and rage, but Vince simply came over and put his foot on Barn's ankle. He pressed down. Pain shot up Barn's leg. He tried to get up, tried to fight, but Vince was too strong and too skilled.

"Leave her alone!" Barn said, his voice coiled and ugly.

"'Leave her alone,'" Vince said, changing his voice into a falsetto. "Leave her alone or I'll huff and puff . . ."

"Just leave her alone," Finn said.

Vince removed his foot, and Barn stood. He wanted to charge Vince again, or take a swing at him, but it was pointless. He knew that. If he could do anything against Vince, it would be with his mind, not his fists.

Barn moved slowly to stand beside Margaret. So did Finn. It was hard to tell with Vince if he was serious or not, if he was truly as aggressive as he seemed. If the beach had been deserted, and no fishermen had been nearby, Vince might do anything. But he was also shrewd and calculating, and Barn saw something wolfish in his expression. He made a mental note never to believe a thing Vince said to him.

"Listen," Barn said, his blood pumping hard, "I'm sorry if I caused you any trouble. I didn't mean to, honestly. We don't want any problems."

"Not your choice," Little Vince said.

That's how Barn thought of him. Little Vince. A shorter, heavier version of Vince. Probably his brother. The third guy, the one with the barbed-wire tattoo around his neck, said nothing at all. He smiled, though, as if he couldn't wait to get started on something. Barn had a sense that any show of weakness from Finn or Margaret or himself would draw them in like hyenas.

"Let's go," Finn said.

Vince stepped closer to Barn. He kept inching closer until his chest was almost against Barn's chest. Barn had never been in a fight. Charging Vince was the first violent action he had ever attempted. He thought fights were stupid, but he also understood maybe it wasn't up to him. That hadn't occurred to him before. You could be peaceful, but other people might not let you be. Vince was the kind of guy who would always be ready to start something.

"We had to pay five hundred dollars to clean up that house," Vince said, his breath touching Barn's cheek. "You better watch your back."

"You shouldn't have egged it," Finn said. Barn wished his friend would stay quiet here.

"I don't like you. I don't like your red hair or your freckles, you hear? You bother me. You've caused me nothing but trouble. Don't come to the beach again. You get me? This is my beach, not yours. You and your little shark friends."

Barn wanted to say something. He didn't know what, but something. Except he was afraid his voice would break out of fear and nervousness.

Vince moved closer and put his chest against Barn's.

"How about it? You want to go?" Vince asked, cocking his head back and forth. He was trying to start the fight. "You took a run at me. I could punch you now, and no one could say a thing. Self-defense."

Margaret stepped in and pushed Vince away.

"Get lost, you loser," she said.

She grabbed Barn by the arm and pulled him toward the road. The barbed-wire-tattoo guy made a sound like a donkey. Little Vince began walking exactly Barn's speed, shoulder to shoulder.

Margaret kept walking, a firm grip on Barn's arm. Finn walked on her other side. Finally, the barbed-wire kid gave up and turned back.

"Keep walking," Margaret whispered. "Don't look around. Just keep walking."

Barn felt unsteady and close to tears. He hated that. He

hated that he had been a chicken. He *knew* it was stupid to fight, but he didn't like how Vince had chested him up. He didn't like how those guys knew they could prey on Margaret and Finn and him.

"Well, that was greasy," Finn said when they had obviously put enough distance between themselves and Vince's boys.

"They are so annoying!" Margaret said.

"I was a chicken. That kid is right."

Margaret shook his arm and turned him to face her.

"They are not worth fighting," she said. "Believe me. They are not worth it. Do you get it? That's all they wanted. You did exactly the right thing. You shouldn't have charged him like that. I had it handled."

Barn had never seen her look so fierce.

He nodded.

Finn, on the other hand, ran forward, jumped in the air, and did a silly-looking karate kick.

"That's terrifying!" Margaret said, slowly laughing. "They would have run away if they had seen your kung fu abilities."

"Owwww," Finn said, standing and rubbing the hip on which he had landed. "That hurt."

"You're such a warrior," Margaret said. "Where did you ever see anyone kick like that in a real fight?"

Barn tried to lighten his mood, but he couldn't manage it. He felt tangled up inside. Someone had called him out, and he had backed down. You could rearrange the facts anyway you liked, but he had let Vince back him down.

"Listen, you guys," he said. "I'm going to call it a night. I'm tired. My ribs still hurt."

"Oh, don't go in yet," Finn said.

Finn threw some more punches. He looked ridiculous.

"It's almost curfew anyway," Margaret said, checking her phone. "You okay, Barn?"

He shrugged. He wasn't sure.

"I'm fine," he said anyway.

"Don't sweat it, buddy," Finn said, and threw an arm over Barn's shoulders. "No biggie. Believe me, though, I would have gone Tasmanian Devil on them."

As soon as Finn dropped his arm from Barn's shoulders,

Margaret stepped in and hugged him. Hard. His entire body tingled. That made a confusing night even more confusing. Barn knew he was supposed to put his arms around her in return. But he only managed to pat her on the shoulder.

"Good night," she said when she pulled away. "Thank you for sticking up for me."

"Good night," Barn answered, his voice squeezed in his throat.

"Later," Finn said.

They did a quick hand-slap thing. It always changed. Finn loved adding new elements. This time it ended with his clapping Barn's hand upside down. Barn could hardly follow it.

Then they took off. They had about a twenty-minute walk. It was almost curfew, but Barn realized his mom was out and Gail had gone to a movie with a friend. He was on his own.

He watched the water a little longer, took a deep breath, then began walking back to Gail's. It wasn't far. And he had only gone a hundred feet before he realized the black

Jeep was driving in the street behind him. They went slow, probably trying to figure out their next move. Barn forced himself not to run, not to show any sign of fear. He had done that already.

He wouldn't do it again.

18

"We can settle this," Vince said.

They were back, and they had him circled. He was alone now. His phone was in his pocket, but that wasn't going to help him. The sun was nearly down. Nobody knew where he was. He couldn't run and didn't want to.

"Settle what?" Barn said. "I have nothing to settle."

"But I do. That's the point. You owe me."

"I don't owe you anything."

Vince did a quick jab step toward him. Barn forced himself not to flinch. But he still did a little. He felt adrenaline climbing through his body.

"Chicken," Little Vince said.

"No, no," Vince said, holding up his hand. "We're friends now. Compatriots, right, Red?"

Barn hated it when people called him Red. But that wasn't the main issue for the moment. The main issue was getting past them without . . .

. . . being a chicken.

"I don't want to play any games with you, Vince. Let's just drop all this."

"We want you to come surfing with us. I do, anyway. Just you and me. You ever go surfing?"

Barn shook his head. What did Vince have in mind? He started to walk away, but the barbed-wire kid shoved him back. Barn felt his face become heated. He wanted to fight, or run, or do something. Any of those choices wouldn't have worked out well. They had him outnumbered.

"Seriously, come on. We'll do a little night surfing. What do you say? We'll play a little game. We'll see who wants to go out farther."

Barn didn't say anything.

"Let's go," Little Vince said.

He shoved Barn, too. Barn tried to stand his ground, but they kept shoving him back down onto the beach. He felt wound up and frightened and angry all at once. Whenever he slowed, or tried to break away, one of Vince's two henchmen shoved him back. It was pointless to resist. He looked for a way to signal a fisherman, or anyone walking the beach, but it was mostly empty now. The only angler was a distant figure sitting on a stool beside his fishing rod. Whatever was going to happen, Barn knew, was going to happen right here and right now.

The barbed-wire kid jogged off and returned with the Jeep. He unloaded two surfboards, probably reclaimed from the police now that the beach had reopened. Barn watched. He had heard about night surfing before. They could do it, and the police would never see them. It was probably pretty cool under the right circumstance. But it was definitely not the right circumstance at this beach right now.

"This is a bad idea," Barn said, his voice unsteady.

"You don't get it. This is the *only* idea. Think of it from our side. We'd love to wreck you, but that would get us in trouble. But if we go surfing with our new pal, Red, why, no one's going to bother about that?"

"Prove you're some big shark expert," Little Vince said. "You can't even surf, you dweeb."

He shoved Barn hard from the side. Barn almost fell, but caught his balance at the last moment. The barbed-wire-tattoo kid shoved him in the other direction. Barn jerked the other way. His ribs ached. His wrist killed.

"A little night surfing, just you and me," Vince said. "Who knows, you might love it, right? It might be your thing. Come on, pal. Let's do it."

Vince had put on a wet suit top. Barn had no idea what to do. He had been on surfboards before, but he wasn't any good at it. He could paddle out okay. Otherwise, he could try to run, or scream, but he realized they would be on him in a second if he did. Besides, he didn't want to think of himself as a chicken. Still, the idea of going in the water at night made him think of . . .

. . . Sweetie Pie.

Or any of Sweetie Pie's cousins. Or even the night in

Apple Way Canal back home when he had fallen into the water and a bull shark had brushed past him twice.

"This is a bad time of year to be out on a surfboard at night," Barn said, trying to keep his voice even. "You should believe me. I know some stuff."

That earned him a shove from barbed-wire guy. And a second shove from Little Vince.

"We'll tell you when it's a good time to be in the water, Red," Vince said. "And now is a good time. Get you stoked. Get your blood going. You're going in the water, so you might as well get used to the idea and take off your shirt at least."

Barn had no options left. He knew they wouldn't let him leave unless he went in the water. Even then, though, he wasn't sure what would happen afterward. He looked back toward the road, but no one noticed this small drama taking place at the water's edge. If anyone had bothered to look, they would have seen a bunch of guys shoving one another and fooling around.

Barn took off his shirt. He folded it and then put his cell phone and wallet inside the fold. He didn't worry about his wallet. He had little money, but his phone was a different matter. They could take that; he had no way to protect it.

Little Vince shoved him as he stood again.

"Okay, okay," Vince said, "let him alone. Let's go, Red. Grab that board. That one's about right for you. Put that tether on. There you go. Now you look like a surfing dude. Doesn't he, boys?"

Barn walked into the water. He didn't want to hear their idiotic words anymore. He didn't care.

The wash of the first wave chilled him to the bone. Barn figured the temperature of the water was somewhere in the low fifties. Pleasant for a quick dip on a hot summer day, but without a wet suit, you didn't want to be in it for more than a minute or two.

"Ready, Red?" Vince said, coming to stand beside him. He had tied his long, scraggly hair behind him in a pony-tail. "We're just two buddies surfing, right? I say the beach is open and that means the beach is open. See? That's how we do it."

Barn looked up and down the line of the beach,

wondering if he could somehow paddle away from them in the near darkness. It didn't seem likely.

He took three steps forward and shoved off on the board. The water stung him with salt and cold. He felt a wild, reckless voice in his head begin to chant.

It's okay, it's okay, it's okay.

That's what the chant said.

And he also thought of the hug Margaret had given him. That was something worth thinking about.

Vince suddenly appeared beside him. It was still light enough to see. Vince made a kind of shout and yell like a dog in pain. Maybe he didn't like the cold. Maybe he wanted to get under Barn's skin. Barn couldn't worry about it, because the first break arced toward him. Not big. Maybe four feet tall, but he had to paddle hard to get up and over the edge.

He did it. That was a small accomplishment.

It's okay, it's okay, it's okay.

Then he chanted something else in his head.

Sweetie Pie, Sweetie Pie, stay away. Sweetie Pie, Sweetie Pie, not today.

He chanted that a dozen times. It never left his head completely.

Now that he was over the first wave, he found himself paddling in a gulley of water. The undertow pulled back and oncoming waves ran forward, and he paddled hard, trying to keep the nose straight and heading into the breaking waves.

But it was cold. Way cold. His teeth chattered. The board was short and easy to manage, but it left part of his legs in the water. A few stars had begun to poke out of the new darkness. The moon had cleared the horizon and sat like a cup spilling water onto the sea.

He paddled hard up the next wave, cleared it, and found himself out where the waves formed in moving mounds of liquid. It *was* exhilarating, he had to admit, but it was also dangerous and stupid. Especially without a wet suit. Especially with . . .

. . . Sweetie Pie on patrol, looking for meals.

Seal meals.

"Woooo-hooooo," Vince yelled.

He had made it, too.

"Now what?" Barn asked.

"You did okay, Red. Not bad. You had more guts than I figured you would."

"I didn't have a choice."

"See any of your shark friends out here?"

"You wouldn't see them until they ate you."

"That's a bunch of noise."

"They hunt from below. If they're in the area right now, they've tracked us. Their hunting skills are a million years old. They hunt at this time of evening especially. In the dim light. Maybe I know a little more about sharks than you do, Vince."

"I know plenty."

"Sweetie Pie is seventeen feet three inches last time she was measured. She's probably bigger now. That's longer than, oh, I don't know, maybe three surfboards lined up. That's what might be under you right now. That's one of the biggest sharks we know in this area. She was here yesterday, right at this beach."

"And you might die in a car crash."

"That's right, Vince. You might. But you don't drive

with your eyes closed, do you? You don't deliberately put yourself in harm's way. You don't know what you're dealing with."

Vince didn't answer. Instead, he reached out and shook Barn's board.

"Scared? Oh, big shark! Woo-woooooooooo."

But Barn heard fear in Vince's voice. That was the way with bullies. Barn was cold and he was on a surfboard in a GWS's strike zone and he wanted to be done with this stupid intimidation.

Vince raised himself up in what Barn's yoga-practicing mom would have called a cobra and scouted the area.

"We've got a rip going," Vince said.

"A rip current?"

"We're going out!" Vince said. "It's taking us right out to sea."

Barn looked around and did the best he could to see what Vince saw. It was true. They were no longer just beyond the breakers. A rip current—a singular movement of water against the bottom contours of the beach—had caused the undertow to become a broom pushing things out to sea. If they had been fifty feet out before, now they were out a hundred.

"Hey! Hey!" Vince yelled to his boys, but they were somewhere in the darkness on the beach. Barn doubted they could hear him. Barn lay still on the board and tried to think. He knew one thing for certain: They were being pushed to the east, out toward Sweetie Pie's favorite seal colony.

19

Barn shivered. He shivered from the cold, and he shivered from unease. This was the world's stupidest thing, and now it had become the most dangerous thing. And it was all Vince's fault.

For a long time neither one of them said anything. They rode their boards and watched the sea rolling toward them in swells of three feet or more. This was what his mother would have called a serious turn of events. That was one of her favorite phrases. Whenever something started to shake apart, she would get a worried look on her face and announce that the situation had become a serious turn of events.

That was certainly the case at the moment. Things had gone from bad to really bad.

"Don't fight the current," Barn said, remembering what he had learned in a swim class when he was eight. "Go parallel to the beach."

"I know that."

"Trouble is, the darker it gets, the harder it will be to see the beach. We could start paddling in the wrong direction."

"We can see lights from the land."

"Maybe. Probably. I'm freezing."

"Then you better paddle," Vince said.

Barn took a deep breath. This was a bad situation. If the cold didn't get him, the sharks might. Barn took a deep breath and tried to use his reasoning faculties. He could outthink a shark, maybe. He certainly couldn't out swim one.

"Listen, Vince, great whites are ambush predators. They like to come at you from behind or below. Sometimes they just come up as hard as they can. That's how most surfers die by shark attack. The shark does a test bite and strikes blood, and then it's all over."

"You have to stop talking about sharks, man. You're freaking me."

"You should be freaked. Paddle carefully. Don't make a bunch of splashes if you can help it. And let's stay together. I mean it. Side by side. Two silhouettes together will be a little confusing to a white. Maybe."

"Seriously, dude, you're freaking me."

Barn closed his eyes. He had to stay calm. When he opened them again, he realized Vince watched him, waiting for the next thing.

"There are a couple hundred sharks in the area at this time of the year. At least. They're all looking for food. We're food. They don't want to hurt you; they just want to eat you. If we're lucky, we can leave the area and they won't bother us. Chances are they won't. But if they do, try to gouge their eyes or gills. They might release you."

"What are you talking about? I'm not gouging eyes."

"That's all you can do. It's your best defense. It's

your only defense, actually. It probably won't work, but it's still worth trying. If it gets you with the first bite, you'll bleed out and that will be that. It will wait outside the kill circle until it can be confident you're dead."

"Come on, let's go. You are one freaky cat, Red."

"Don't call me Red, either. My name is Barn."

"Whatever," Vince said, and started to paddle.

Barn did his best, but Vince paddled faster. Barn shouted at him to slow down. Barn was aware his voice had become shaky from the cold and from the entire situation. Adrenaline. Fear. Vince let him catch up. Barn's ribs killed him.

"Stay together. It's a better silhouette."

"What are you talking about with all this silhouette stuff?"

"From below. From the shark's point of view."

Vince raised up again on his board.

"We're a long way out," he said.

"At least we can see the lights. You were right about that."

"I heard about a surfer who was picked up by a tanker five miles off the coast. He had been dragged out."

"That's not helpful right now," Barn said.

"I mean, we can make it, anyway."

For a time, all he felt was water and wind and salt. And approaching darkness. The sea kept rolling waves at him like someone shaking out a blanket on a bed to get it to settle without wrinkles. Barn realized there were no gulls to keep him company. They had gone to roost. Or to nest. Or to wherever gulls spent the night.

"This is a big rip," Vince said.

His voice sounded strange after so much silence. Barn had to force himself to come out of his own thoughts.

"Have you been in one before?" he asked.

"Once."

"Did you survive?"

It was a joke, but Barn saw Vince frown, trying to figure it out. Barn let it go.

"How far out do you think we are?" he asked.

"Quarter mile. A little less."

"We should go west, away from the seals."

"We are."

Then Barn heard Vince ask something he could hardly believe.

"You okay?" asked Vince.

"I'm cold."

"I figured that."

"Hypothermia can set in pretty fast. If we don't get in soon . . . ," Barn trailed off.

"I know, dude."

"Keep paddling."

Barn felt better when he paddled, but he was aware his strokes had lost some strength from the cold. Cold water could kill you more dependably than a great white. He knew that. Vince pulled ahead again. Barn told him to slow down. He heard his voice had gone croaky with cold. Barn felt his chest had gone raw from rubbing against the rough texture of the surfboard. His ribs felt as if they stabbed his chest with each paddle.

"What was that?" Vince asked when Barn pulled beside him.

"What was what?"

"I thought I saw a fin. I swear."

"Are you making that up?"

"No, honest."

"It could have been anything."

"It could have been, but I'm telling you I saw a fin."

"You're just getting freaked."

"I'm telling you."

"People don't really see fins that often. Sharks don't make a habit of swimming with their fins out of the water."

"You trying to tell me I didn't see what I saw? I saw a fin!"

"It doesn't matter anyway. We can't do anything about it. Stay together. A big silhouette is better than a small, single silhouette. I promise. We'll be okay."

But Barn wasn't sure they would be okay.

He lifted his torso from the board and looked around. It was almost completely dark now. Vince had been right about one thing—they could see the land lights without a problem. When the waves swelled beneath them, he could see the lights easily. Barn wasn't sure Vince had actually seen a fin. It was possible, but unlikely. Eyes played tricks on you at night. What Vince saw as a fin could have been a piece of debris or a strange turn of water.

Barn wondered, too, if he was still thinking clearly. Hypothermia could make you delusional. Even with a wet suit, Vince might be affected. Maybe they were both loopy. All he could do was paddle. But his shoulders and arms ached. His ribs caught his lungs or something inside. He wasn't accustomed to paddling. The cold water sucked his heat away. It also made him weaker.

They had paddled another twenty yards or so, Barn figured, when he saw the fin. It was a big fin. It was difficult to see in the darkness, but it was unquestionably a fin. It cleared the water maybe fifteen feet away. Barn reached over and touched Vince's board.

"There's a shark here," he said calmly.

"I told you!"

"Stay calm. There's nothing we can do but be as smart as possible. You can't outpaddle it and you can't scare it away. We're in its environment. Stay close together and don't splash. Lift your limbs out of the water as much as possible."

"This is bad," Vince whispered.

Barn flexed his knees so that his legs were out of the water. Vince did, too. For a long time, they didn't paddle, didn't move. Barn kept his left hand on Vince's board so that the silhouette they projected to the ocean bottom was wide and uninteresting. A piece of driftwood. An old barrel. Anything but food.

Silence covered them. Barn had never felt a silence like this one. It felt like the silence in movies when a girl or boy goes down the basement steps and you knew, *you knew,* that something was about to jump out from the darkness.

That silence.

The fin had disappeared, but that didn't mean anything, Barn understood. In the darkness, he couldn't be certain it was a great white. Basking sharks sometimes passed by Cape Cod, he knew. They were gentle creatures with large fins. It could have been a dolphin or even a seal's flipper. It could have even been a mola mola, an enormous sunfish that could grow to nine feet and frequently visited the waters off Cape Cod. If it was a GWS, they could be toast. It was up to the shark.

"We're out of the rip," Vince whispered. "We're being pulled back to shore."

"Good."

"This is the freakiest thing . . ."

"It's like walking across a frozen lake and you're not sure the ice will hold. You could go through on any step."

Barn didn't know where that came from. But it was true.

"Sorry," Vince said. "Sorry that I forced you out here."

"It was a bad idea."

"I know. Sorry."

Barn nodded.

"My skin is tingling," Barn said.

"Mine too."

"It's a defensive reaction. The body is preparing for flight or fight."

"I can't believe this is happening."

"The sharks are here. We knew that."

"But we didn't know one was . . ."

Then a sound came from deep below. It came like the sound of something falling through space, something getting faster and faster and faster.

Barn held his hand tight on Vince's surfboard. He lifted his legs a little higher away from the water.

Then something exploded.

Something large and heavy and wildly alive.

The world became a wild, spinning snow globe. Water splashed up and caught the rays of the moon, and Barn realized it was a beautiful thing, this heartbeat of death, this attack that had come not more than ten feet away from them both!

Barn turned and saw the last of the attack.

It *was* a GWS. And it had just torn a seal in half.

Barn saw a second spray of water from the shark's swirl. Whatever had happened had happened quickly. The shark had stalked the seal and then had come up and caught the seal in jaws that could deliver close to four thousand pounds of pressure. The seal had sliced open like a grape.

Barn heard the seal grunt. It was a deep, painful grunt.

An instant later, Barn smelled blood.

He *smelled* it. That was an incredible thing. It changed the air around him and made everything warmer. Barn didn't know if that was possible, that blood could make the air warmer, but it felt like it. Close and humid. It smelled like metal.

Barn knew what would happen next. If the shark had succeeded in fatally biting a seal, it would lie back and wait, letting the seal bleed out into the water. There was no need to rush. The shark did not want to risk injury, and once the seal had lost sufficient blood, the shark would close on it and begin eating it. If it had been daylight, seagulls would have already been on the water, searching for scraps. But it was night, and the water smelled of blood.

"It made a kill," Barn whispered.

"I can't see it."

"I can smell it."

"So can I."

"Stay clear of the area. Paddle away."

"It's close, though. We're almost next to it."

"I know. The good news is, it probably won't bother us now. It will concentrate on the seal."

"There it is!" Vince said, his voice almost twisting in a knot.

Suddenly the shark swam at the seal. Its enormous fin was unmistakable in the dim light. Great white shark. Despite his fear, despite the cold, Barn felt himself tingle with excitement. A GWS! It wasn't more than fifteen feet away. He knew a GWS did not bite and chew. It locked its jaws on its prey and shook until the flesh tore away, often as much as thirty pounds in a single bite. Barn listened. A moment later, he heard severe splashing. The shark had gone back to the seal and had begun to feast. The water churned.

"It's on it," Barn said. "It's eating it."

"There's blood in the water. It's everywhere. My hands are red."

"We're in its kill circle. We need to get away."

"We can head in now. The water is working with us."

"I'm really cold," Barn said.

"So am I, but stay with it."

Barn felt a little hazy. He also felt incredibly interested in watching the GWS devour the seal. Depending on the size of the seal, it wouldn't take long. Maybe five bites. Maybe ten. Then a thought occurred to him. It was a distant thought, half-formed, but important. He tried to call it to the front of his mind, but it lingered back in the fog from the cold.

"Other sharks might show up," he said once he had finally snagged the thought. "When they smell blood."

"Don't tell me anything else about sharks, will you?"

"It's better to know than to not know."

"Paddle. I can't take it."

Barn felt his strength giving out. He had begun to shiver harder. They were not the shivers that came from being out on a skating pond in the middle of a winter afternoon. They were serious shakes, his body telling him he needed to get into the warmth. Any warmth. He found it harder and harder to keep his thoughts lined up. Everything hurt. Shoulders, arms, ribs, wrists.

Then something miraculous happened.

The shark swam beside him. For a fleeting moment, the shark came close, swimming past Barn's ocean side. It went in the same direction as Barn went. He forced himself to go into scientist mode, despite the waves of confusion that the cold had put in his brain. He rose up on the board and tried to estimate the height of the fin, the distance between the dorsal fin and the caudal fin. It was difficult to do in the darkness, in the water at a level with the shark, but Barn concluded that the shark was huge. Seventeen feet, at least. Maybe more. It was like being passed by a small school bus.

Then he heard more thrashing. That quickly, the shark had returned to its kill. Maybe it had wanted to check the surfboards out to make sure they were not invading sharks, coming to collect food from the kill. Regardless, it was time to paddle, to make progress. The shark had examined them and found nothing of interest for the moment.

"Let's go," Barn said. "Paddle hard."

"I thought you said we shouldn't splash."

"We have to get in," Barn said, but that was all his brain could manage.

Barn tasted salt on his lips. His arms felt like lead weights. His shoulders burned. But he paddled. Now the water began to carry them toward land. He did not know if he could make it. His skin felt hot, suddenly, and he almost wanted to roll into the water to cool off. A weary part of his mind reminded him that heat was one of the final signs of hypothermia. Sometimes people who succumbed to hypothermia were found naked in the snow, their internal furnaces hot with the final push of heat from their dying bodies.

"The next wave," Vince said.

"What next wave?"

"The next wave. We can ride it. It will take us in."

"We saw a shark," Barn said, confused.

"I know we saw a shark, dude. Wake up. You tracking with me?"

"Cold."

"Just a little more. A little more and we'll be in. Stay with it."

Barn nodded, even though he wasn't sure what Vince meant. The heat had started to boil inside him. He wanted to dunk in the water. He wanted to cool down. Then Vince shook his board.

"You don't have to stand up or anything. Just paddle and catch the wave. Stay on your belly. Wake up, man. You're fading."

"I'm okay."

"Are you? Come on. Turn the nose of your board toward shore. Ready? Come on. Not this wave, the next one. That's a good one. Just start paddling when I say to go. Hold on to your board tight once you get into the wave, okay? Stay with it for two more minutes."

Barn knew what he was supposed to do, but he wasn't sure he could carry it off. Then he heard something. It was his mother's voice. At first he thought that was kind of weird, kind of like hearing a mermaid sing. Then he realized it *was* his mother's voice. She was calling from the beach, shouting out into the darkness. He tried to call back, but his voice failed. Nothing worked very well anymore. He heard Vince's friends calling, too. Their voices sounded like a bass line under his mother's calling.

"Now," Vince said. "Paddle!"

Barn did his best, but his arms slapped the water ineffectively. He felt the wave build beneath him. He began to lift, to see the beach, and he listened for his mother's voice. The wave caught him and began to churn over his legs. Then he felt a momentary exhilaration of riding a wave. He had boogie boarded before, but this was different. The board was stiffer, for one thing, and it pulled ahead like someone yanking you onto the dance floor.

The wave broke. It crashed over him and Barn tried to hold on, he truly tried, but the wave twisted him away. The board went down and the tether on his ankle pulled him toward the bottom. He knew it couldn't be too deep. They were not far from shore and he tried to grab the tether and climb it back to the board, but his strength had given out.

"There you are, there you are!" he heard someone say next to his ear. "I've got you now."

It was Jessup Sabine. He stood waist-deep in the water. Barn tried to figure out how that had happened, what it meant, but his mind had stopped functioning properly. He felt himself lifted and felt another wave hit them from behind, but Jessup had him, he had promised, and that was okay with Barn.

21

Just before waking, Barn saw the shark again.

It swam beside him in a dream. It spy-hopped—twisted in the water and looked at him directly, a behavior GWS's did to check seals on land—and asked in a calm voice, *How ya doing, Barn?*

Okay, Barn answered.

Nice meeting you.

You too.

See you down the road.

Keep swimming, Barn ended.

Then he woke.

He was in a hospital. A white room. He wondered if Sweetie Pie hadn't gotten him after all. He looked up fast and checked his limbs. All there. He moved his hand around his body to check it. Then he realized his mother sat next to the bed, and she reached out her hand and grabbed his.

"It's okay," she said quietly. "You're in for hypothermia. You're okay. You're out of danger now."

"Where am I?"

"A clinic. It's a Cape Cod clinic in Barnstable, I think. I'm not entirely sure. I came with you in the ambulance."

She stood up and bent over him. She touched the sides of his head with her hands. Barn loved looking in his mom's eyes.

"You cannot end up in the water with any more sharks! Do you hear me, Barn? You stay out of the water."

"I didn't mean to."

She kissed his forehead and pushed back his hair.

"I know. Vince told us the whole story."

"Is he . . . ?"

"He's fine. You're both fine. He's already been released

from the hospital, but he's being held by the police. He had the wet suit so he didn't feel the cold the way you did."

"How did you know where I was?"

She smiled.

"Didn't you know? Mothers have a lateral line connected to their kids. Wherever the kids go, the mother knows. I'm a mama shark."

"No, seriously."

She sat back down and took his hand. She squeezed it.

"When we got back—"

"From your date," Barn interrupted.

She nodded.

"Okay, from our date. You weren't there. You didn't leave a note, and when I tried to text you, there was no answer. Gail hadn't come home yet, so we called Margaret and Finn. They told us what had happened on the beach . . . how Vince and his friends had surrounded you. So we went to the beach to check, and the two boys, Vince's friends, they told us what had happened. They couldn't see you from shore. No one could. We thought the worst had happened."

"I'm sorry, Mom."

"It wasn't your fault, Barn."

"Maybe I should get another hobby," he said. "Study porcupines instead."

"Maybe you should," she said, and rose to kiss him again. "Some people are outside and want to say hello. Do you feel strong enough?"

He nodded. He felt his body returning to him. That was an odd way to think of it, but it was true. The tingling that had buzzed in his limbs, the deep, shuddering cold that had come up from his backbone, had now subsided. It felt good to be in the warmth. It felt spectacular to be out of the water.

Margaret was the first person to enter. She wore a hoodie and a pair of pj bottoms and huge slippers on her feet. She stood for a second at the foot of the bed, then zoomed around and hugged him. It was awkward. He had never been hugged by anyone in front of his mother. In fact, he had only been hugged by Margaret three times. This was the third total—the second time in a day!

"You gave us such a scare!" she said, pulling back.

"I know."

His tongue felt thick with Margaret next to the bed.

Then Finn came in and did an elaborate handshake that Barn tried to copy. Finn bent down and hugged him, too, when the handshake finished.

"Dude," Finn said, and shook his head. "You and sharks, man. You got some weird connection there."

"We saw one take a seal."

"Vince said," Finn said. "He's here if you want to talk to him. The police are making him apologize. That's part of his punishment. He might be charged with kidnapping. He's in a lot of trouble, so you don't have to talk to him unless you want to."

"I guess so."

"I'll go get him," Finn said.

Jessup came in then. Barn took Jessup's good hand.

"Thank you," Barn said.

"No thanks needed."

Barn looked straight into Jessup's eyes. They traded some sort of understanding, but Barn wasn't sure in that instant that he understood what it was. But he knew it was good. He knew he and Jessup were solid.

Vince came in and stood at the foot of the bed. He looked shame-faced. Officer Calhoun stood in the doorway. Vince kept his eyes down at the floor. He didn't look up at all.

"Sorry," Vince said. He mumbled. Barn could barely hear him.

Barn nodded.

Then Officer Calhoun stepped close to Vince and whispered something to him. Vince nodded but didn't lift his eyes from the floor. He moved around the bed, and Margaret and Barn's mom stepped back.

"I'm sorry, Barn. We could have been killed. Forget the shark, we could have been killed by the rip tide."

"I guess so," Barn said.

"Sometimes I just do things and I don't know why I do them. It's stupid, but that's the way it is. I can't help myself."

Vince left immediately after his apology. Officer Calhoun walked him out.

Barn's mom sat down beside the bed again.

"I hate that boy," she said. "I shouldn't hate anyone, but I hate that boy."

"Hurt people hurt people," Barn said, which was a line she always used. It meant people who were broken tried to break other people.

She nodded.

"Am I going home tonight?" he asked.

"No, tomorrow. You'll sleep all night right here where they can monitor you. You've had quite an experience."

Barn turned to Jessup.

"It was about fourteen feet," he said. "Huge. Maybe even bigger. I'm trying not to exaggerate."

"Could have been Sweetie Pie," Jessup said.

Barn nodded. He felt himself getting sleepy. It was good to be in bed. It was good to be warm. It was good when Margaret put her hand on his arm and said good night. He wondered if they had given him something to make him sleep. He thought of the water. He thought of the smell of blood and the shark gliding past. He thought of the color of the moonlight on the water as it boiled up in the wake of the attack. Then he let go and climbed down off the surfboard, and it wasn't water this time, but sleep. He sank into it, and nothing had ever felt any better.

Barn woke afraid.

For a moment, he didn't know where he was.

White room, he thought.

White room. He thought maybe it was Gail's house, then remembered he was in some sort of clinic in Barnstable, Massachusetts. He closed his eyes for a second, wondering if he had been dreaming, wondering if Sweetie Pie had jetted by in his dream, but then he realized someone stood at the foot of his bed. He thought of his dad. His dad had spent a summer on Cape Cod. His mom and dad had met not far from where he was right now. That seemed strange and a little magical. But his dad couldn't be beside his bed. His dad lived on the *Dog Bite* for a summer. That wasn't near his bed.

Barn woke a little more.

"Vince?" he asked.

Maybe Vince had come back. Maybe. Maybe Vince had another trick to play.

"Not Vince," the voice said. "Sorry. Didn't mean to wake you."

"Who are you? Are you a nurse?"

"No, sorry."

It was a young man. He came around the bed. Barn didn't recognize him.

"My name is Dimitri Xanthopoulous. My brother was killed on Wellfleet Beach."

Barn pushed the sleep out of his eyes. He made the connection instantly.

"I recognize the name."

"I heard about what happened to you. Out on the water. I don't know why, but I wanted to talk to you. Not many people you can talk to about being in the water with a great white shark."

Barn nodded. He understood. It was why, strangely, he felt fellowship with Vince, despite Vince being the cause of it all. They had gone through something together. Bonded. That's what Dimitri was talking about.

"Have a seat," Barn said. "What time is it?"

"It's late. I just finished at the parlor. My dad, he runs a pizza parlor. Are you hungry? I brought a pie in case you were."

Barn *was* hungry. In fact, he was famished. He pulled the little bedside eating tray closer, and Dimitri slid a pie on top of it.

"It's good pizza," Dimitri said, sitting. "Help yourself. I won't join you because I am completely sick of pizza by this time in the summer. I cook pizza all day, every day. I'm sick of it, honest."

Barn took a slice. It was big and floppy, the way he liked it. He folded it and stabbed it toward his mouth. He was surprised that he missed by a little. His hand was still shaky.

Dimitri handed him a napkin.

"The fin was so big," Dimitri said. "Sometimes I think about how big it was. It still makes me wake up sometimes. I can see it in the water, moving like a knife cutting something. The whole thing."

"I'm sorry about your bother."

Dimitri smiled. He didn't speak for a moment. Barn realized he had to collect himself, that the death of his brother was far from finished with him.

"He was a great kid. We fought sometimes like brothers do, but we loved each other. I miss him every day."

"Sorry. It's a terrible loss."

Dimitri smiled and let out a big sigh.

"Not your fault. Not anyone's fault. Just nature and bad luck. I don't hate sharks. I really don't. I've given money to a fund that does research on them. It does me good to do that. Helps me let go of my anger. The shark wasn't being mean to Jimmy. He was just doing what he does."

Barn nodded. He admired Dimitri's attitude.

"What I came by for was just to tell you if you ever want to talk to someone, you know, someone who was in the water with a shark, then you should call me. Anytime, day or night. And if you don't mind, I'll call you, too, if I need to. Would that be okay?"

"Sure. Of course."

"I mean, that shark was huge and so . . ."

"So alive," Barn filled in for him.

"Incredibly alive. You realize in the ocean nothing is slow. It all happens fast. Animals have to fight or run . . . it's all fast."

Barn nodded. He chewed his pizza. It was delicious.

"I saw you on that news program. You're interested in sharks," Dimitri said. "Is that true?"

"Yes."

"Well, good. They need good people to help them."

"If you don't mind me asking, what happened to the surfboard?"

"We burned it. We made a bonfire on the beach where the accident occurred. I have a picture on my phone, though. Do you want to see it?"

"Are you sure?"

Dimitri nodded. He pulled out his phone, scrolled through some pictures, then handed the phone to Barn. Barn examined the board. The shark had taken part of the rear portion of the surfboard, which made Barn conclude that it had been a test bite. Probably. He wouldn't know for sure. No one would.

"Jimmy's picture is there, too. Next one or two. See him? He was a good kid. A really good kid."

Barn looked at the pictures. It was sad to think the boy was gone. Barn handed the phone back to Dimitri. What was there to say?

"Sorry," he said, knowing that was inadequate.

Dimitri sighed again. He opened the pizza box.

"Maybe one slice," he said.

They ate for a few minutes without speaking. Then Barn had an idea.

"You like the Sox?"

"Love the Sox," Dimitri said.

"They put the replay on late night. You want to watch an inning or two?"

"You're not too sleepy?"

"No, I feel wide awake. Use the remote there."

"I know the channel," Dimitri said, flicking the set on. "They're not that good this year."

"It's not over yet. Nothing's over yet," Barn said.

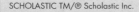